# BLOOD MOON

# Blood Moon

#ITS ONLY BLOOD

#NO SHAME

# Lucy Cuthew

Walker Books

Copyright © 2020 by Lucy Cuthew

First US paperback edition 2022

Library of Congress Catalog Card Number 2020912891
ISBN 978-1-5362-1503-8 (hardcover)
ISBN 978-1-5362-2578-5 (paperback)

21 22 23 24 25 26 TRC 10 9 8 7 6 5 4 3 2 1

Printed in Eagan, MN, USA

This book was typeset in Plantin Infant MT.

Walker Books US
a division of
Candlewick Press
99 Dover Street
Somerville, Massachusetts 02144

www.walkerbooksus.com

**For
Bronwen,
Helen,
Kirsten,
and
Rachel**

# PART
# ONE

# A Slice of Night

I perch on the bench in
the planetarium staff room
and take out my phone,
with its smooth black-and-gold
star-spangled case, and
read all the messages
from today while I wait
listening to the silent room,
checking it's empty
before I get changed.

There's a message from Dad
and a ton in the chat
with the girls called
PEANUT BUTTER AND JELLY
(the only thing
any of us can make).

**Dad**
I will be the one in the
white ford behind the trees
at five past zero
hundred hours. D x

    I think he's being *funny*,
    but I don't get it.

He's on another planet.
At least he's agreed
to pick me and Harriet up
out back,
and not INSIDE
the ice rink,
like he wanted to.


I open PEANUT BUTTER AND JELLY.


**Harriet**
Just getting ready!!


**Bethany**
Remind me why we're going
to an *ICE-RINK* birthday party.
Are we ten again?


**Leylah**
Apparently it's free cuz
Jackson's on the ice hockey team,
but it's totally so he can show
off to everybody.


**Harriet**
He can show off to me.
Apparently he's amazing.


**Bethany**
I thought you liked Lee?


**Harriet**
I can multitask.

**Bethany**

Ha.

I'm secretly into it.

**Marie**

I'm openly into it.

It'll be fun.

**Harriet**

What you all wearing?

**Leylah**

Shorts and a crop top . . .

And a giant hoodie,

to get past the parental police.

**Marie**

Erm . . . Ley, *ICE* skating . . .

I'm wearing two pairs of leggings

and three shirts

under my sweater.

**Leylah**

Ugh. Changing now.

Warm clothes are so

unflattering on me.

At least I'll be allowed out.

**Harriet**

You always look lovely.

Has anyone heard

from Frankie today?

**Me**
I'm here!
Just finishing work.
Tell me when
you're there. XX

I finish typing,
then take off my uniform
and let my dress
slink down over my
not-completely-flat
(but also not-yet-
satisfactory) chest.

A dab of concealer,
a pump of face mist:
I'm good to go.

*Jackson Twigger's
Sweet Sixteenth
at the ice rink.*

(Although . . .
Jackson Twigger.
*Sweet?*
LOL.)

While I wait for the girls,
I scroll through my phone.
Harriet's posted a photo
of herself in our tree house.
#GettingReady #InstaMakeup

#Starlight #StarGazing #NightsOut
She looks really pretty,
her eyes all smoky,
but I know
the photo
is from
ages ago.

It shouldn't annoy me,
but we're *not* getting ready
in our tree house tonight,
and I hate when
she's being fake.

Under the photo
Jackson's replied,
"ur hot."

Harriet's written
"thanks babe" and
added a winky face.

(Does she actually *like* him
or does she just like flirting?)

**Harriet**
We're here!
Bring it, beeatch.

I pull on my sneakers,
then open the door
to the atrium,

where Vidhi is
putting away a wooden box
of sparkling meteor rocks.

I wish I'd waited here
talking to her
about astronomy
instead of looking
at what Harriet's posting.

"Have a good time,"
Vidhi says.
"You were great today.
You're clearly
really
into this."

"Thanks," I say,
her compliment
blazing inside me
incandescently.

"Don't forget to send me
your application for the
summer program.
Or you can
just bring it
next Saturday.
I'll make sure
Elaine gets it."

"I won't forget," I say,
a flutter of nerves
at the thought of her

and the director
of this whole place
reading my essay.
"Thanks, Vidhi,
see you Saturday."

"I'll be rooting for you!"
she says,

which means
the World

to me.

(Vidhi did the exact same
summer program when
she was sixteen,
and now she's got a
PhD in Astronomy.
#LifeGoals)

I push open
the double doors
and breathe in
the streetlight night.
Over the buildings,
the crescent moon
is a sharp, bright slice
of otherworldly light.

I snap a quick picture.
The moon comes out tiny,
all of its majesty
lost by my phone's
complete inability
to take a picture of something

so far from me.
I know Harriet
will find it funny.

**Me**
Took this and thought of you.
#ShitPicturesOfTheMoon

**Harriet**
LOL. Get your ass in here.
Skating's starting soon.

# Sweet Sixteen

"Frankie!" Harriet screams,
waving at me,
bracelets jangling,
as I walk into the chilly
and unnecessarily
brightly lit room.

The music is loud,
and our crowd
spills out of a booth
near the rental skates.
I climb over the back
of the seats
and slide in
between Harriet and Marie.

Jackson is already strutting
in front of the group,
talking loudly,
as though we're
his own personal audience.

There's Bethany,
            Leylah,
             Marie,
             Me,
             Harriet (laughing loudly),
             Dev,
          Lee,
and Charlie.

Jackson is telling everyone
how last weekend
he got a new mountain bike
on his actual birthday.

Then went out riding
and met two girls
who were all over him
because
　　　*babes love bikes.*

Then he tells us how
he ended up banging
them both
as a birthday present.

　　　　　　　　　(Yeah, right.)

He shows us all
a picture of him
straddling his bike,
with two girls kissing him,
one on each cheek.

　　　　　　"How long do we
　　　　　have to listen to this?"
　　　　　I mutter to Harriet,

but she doesn't
answer me,

and Jackson is still going,
gesticulating grotesquely
with his overmobile groin.

Harriet grins at me
and fans her crotch,
then rolls her eyes
like she's about to faint.

I whisper to Marie,
"Is it just me,
or is Jackson disgusting?"

but Marie's not listening.

Then Jackson looks at me,
scathingly.
Maybe he heard me.
I hope he did.
I don't care if he hates me.

Harriet's eyes stay
fixed on him.
Then she laughs
at something he says,
and throws back her head,
like a wolf howling at the moon.

As she does,
her tilted-up chin
leaves a gap and
I notice someone I hadn't
previously seen:
        Benjamin Jones.

He's sitting between
Dev and Lee

in a leather jacket,
looking explosively hot.

He turns his eyes to me,
and right then
*something physical*
happens
down below.

He's so good-looking
I can feel the photons
bouncing off him
and colliding
with me.
#InstantCrush

# Noticing

The next time Harriet laughs,
my and Benjamin's eyes meet
in the tiny bit of space-time
her thrown-back head creates.

I smile at him slightly.
He smiles back at me.

I don't know when
we last spoke,
but recently I have noticed him
noticing me.

Only now it's not just
noticing each other,
or looking at each other.
We're really
seeing each other.

# Blushing

"What are you
blushing about?"
Harriet's whisper
is like sandpaper
on my eardrum.

"I'm not!"
I say, my voice high,
my larynx tight.

I thought she
was too busy
watching Jackson
to notice the color
of my cheeks, but

she's staring at me,
a single raised eyebrow
grilling me.

My cheeks grow redder
under the heat.

I could tell her
I'm giving Benjamin
the eye,

but I prefer
the privacy of
realizing

*I like Benjamin*
and not telling her.

I usually tell her
everything.

"Fine, ignore me,"
she says, climbing over me.
"I'm going to talk to Lee
while my hair still
looks amazing."

(Which one is it?
Jackson or Lee?)

Then she leans back in.
"By the way,
    Blushing Fact:
    apparently
    it's not just your cheeks
    the blood rushes to
    when you're embarrassed.

It's your lady lips too."
            She nods at my crotch
                and grins,

                    and I whack her.
                    "Harriet! Yuck!
                You make everything
                    disgusting!"

"That's why you love me,"
she says

as she leaps off the bench,
sticks the landing,
and flicks her hair back
like she knows
she looks amazing.

Her skirt is hitched up.
Stuck on her tights,

and I try to tell her,
but the music is so loud.

And anyway,
right then I catch
Benjamin's eye again
and am presented,
instantly,
with confirmation
of her blushing fact.

# Milkshake

Harriet squeezes onto
the end of the bench,
leans in to whisper
something to Lee,
and pushes Benjamin
one person closer to me.
I listen to him
chatting to Dev,
wondering how
I can join in.

Then the waitress
brings our shakes.
No one can remember
who ordered which flavor,
so she dumps them all
in the middle
and everyone *l e a n s*
across the table,
      milkshake spilling
      and finger licking.

I scrunch up my face
at the stickiness
and pull my elbows away
from the mess.
Harriet catches me,
rolls her eyes at me.

Then pulls the last shake
slowly toward herself, saying,
"O-o-o, Oreo,
o-o-o how I love you-eo!"

"Really," says Marie,
sarcastically.
"You've never mentioned it."

Harriet picks an Oreo
out of the shake
and swivels off
the top cookie
so she can lick the filling.

She shrugs as she says,
"I know what I like."

Then Jackson leans in and says,
    "Want mine?"
    and picks the Oreo
      off the top of his shake,
      twists one cookie off
      and, leaving a trickle
      of chocolate syrup
        across the table,
          offers it to Harriet
          to lick the cream.

I turn to Marie,
so I don't have to see
Harriet's tongue
near Jackson's fingers.
    (It's so unnecessary,

the
flirty,
touchy,
licky,
publicness
of what they're doing.)

When I look back,
Dev's getting up,
and
Benjamin
is
right next to me.

I sip my milkshake,
wondering how
to talk to him,
without anyone
*noticing*.

And even though it's obscene,
I can't help wondering whether
he's watching as
I put my lips to my straw
and suck.

And there I go again.
I'm blushing,
but just then

Benjamin's arm
brushes my elbow

and I'm just about
to speak, when

the music gets louder

and Jackson shouts,
"Let's do this!"

Everyone gets up
to go and get rental skates,
and our moment
is broken.

# On the Ice

Us girls
do swooping laps
under the disco ball,
which draws circles,
shedding sparkles
in time with the beat.

We laugh at the boys
who can't all skate,
and watch Jackson
zigzag backward,
like the show-off he is,
pulling Harriet after him,
holding her hands,
her hair flying behind her
and her laughter erupting
in flirty explosions
over the music.

And

*a l l    n i g h t ,*
I try to get
near Benjamin.

Then,
before midnight,
the lights turn low,
and a slow
song comes on

and there he is,
in front of me.

"Hey," I say,
over the bass.
"How are you?"

"Good, thanks,"
he says,
sliding closer.
"You?"

"Good," I say.

Then he slips
and wobbles a bit
and his hand shoots
out,
so I take his fingers
in my palm,
helping him
balance.

We're skin-to-skin.
His hand is warm.
And I'm worried
I'm going to say
something stupid,
or weird,

which is weird,
because *stupid*
is *so* not my thing,

so I say,
"Shall we skate?"

He nods and gives me
a sheepish grin.
"Sure thing."

And we drift apart a little bit
as we circle the rink,
and before I know it,
we're talking,
and it's so easy.

"Do you usually come here
on Saturday nights?"

"No!" I say, laughing.
"I work at the planetarium,
then usually I go home,
and Dad makes me
and Mom a pizza
and we have
movie night."

"Nice."

"What about you?
What do you
normally do?"

"Not this!" he says,
slipping again
and tightening his grip

on my hand.
"I play rugby with a
club team on Sunday mornings,
so I just get
an early night."

"Wild," I say, smiling
while trying to stop
picturing me and him
having a wild night in.

"If I don't have rugby,
and I'm feeling really crazy,
I sometimes stay up
until, like, midnight,
watching science stuff online."

"What kind of
stuff do you like?"

"Space stuff," he says.
"Mostly. Some of it
is so amazing."

I want to whisper,
*You're amazing*,
but instead I say,
"Yeah, amazing."

# Dark

**It's as
dark
as night
on the ice.**

And in the darkness,
no one can see
what you're doing,
or thinking.
And that
makes me
bold.

I slide along beside him,
our fingers touching,
and just like that
we're holding hands.

I look around,
quickly checking
if anyone is looking,
but Harriet is with Jackson,
pushing Dev into Marie,
being so obvious it's embarrassing.
She doesn't see me.

The disco ball
rotates above us.
His face is speckled
with the silver flecks

of the turning light.

I want to say,
"I like your face,"
but instead I just blush
and breathe in

his leather jacket
and something sweet,
like

"Cherry ChapStick?"

"Huh?" he says.

"Are you wearing
lip balm?"

Benjamin chuckles
and takes my arm,
to draw me closer.
"Yes," he whispers.
"But don't tell anyone.
It's my sister's."

"Why are you
wearing it, then?"
I tease.

"Because it's cold
and I've got chapped lips
and she left it
in my pocket."

"You share clothes with
your sister?"

He laughs. "We're close,"
he says and shrugs.

"And it's a great jacket."

"It is," I say,
laughing as we

lap the rink,
our arms going slack and taut
pulling each other closer and
drifting away because of

*centrifugal force.*

"Huh?" he shouts.
"What did you say?"

"Nothing."
I shake my head.
My hair flies out behind me.
I feel like Beyoncé.

"You did!" he says,
pulling me close again.
"You said *centrifugal.*"

"Well, it is," I say, laughing,
although strictly speaking
*centrifugal* is a fictitious force,
a mere explanation of a sensation.
But the music's too loud
to go into that now.

He laughs and suddenly
brakes with his skates,
swinging me around him,
demonstrating he
knows exactly

what I mean
by *centrifugal*.

I take his other hand
and twirl around him.

We stay like that
for what feels like
an eternity,
staring at each other,
until he pulls me in
and—

in my mind
the word

KIS **S** ING

explodes like a neutron star
leaving a black hole,
sucking everything in.
I'm freezing.
I don't know how to *do*
this kind of *kissi*—

Then suddenly
the disco ball halts,
the music stops.
Our hands drop.

Midnight strikes.
The magic disperses.
And in the flight to escape
the bright electric light,
I lose Benjamin.

# Smelly Feet

We're just changing our shoes
when Benjamin
comes up to me.

"Hey," he says.

       "Hey," I say, hoping the smell
           from my socked feet
           isn't wafting his way.
           (I've been at work all day.)

"I've got to go,
but it was fun
skating with you.
Thanks for helping me."

       I want to say something
           smart or witty,
           but I don't know *what*.

       "Yeah," I say, "it was, um . . ."

"Centrifugal?" he offers.

       I laugh, impressed,
       and a bit annoyed
       he got there first.

"You're great on skates,
by the way,"

he says, then grins
and walks away.

Leaving Harriet,
Marie, Bethany, and Leylah
staring at me.

# Benjamin Likes Me?

We say goodbye to the other girls.
I walk out next to Harriet,
with smelly feet,
on cloud nine.

As we weave under
the lit-up parking lot trees
to meet my dad,
Harriet goes on and on
about who likes who
and how Jackson
is so much nicer
when you talk to him
one-on-one.

Then she blabs on
about how Marie and Dev
would make a cute pair
if only they weren't both
so shy and how she's
going to try
and help Marie by getting
her to send Dev a
flirty selfie.

"Maybe I should do it for her?"

"No," I say. "Don't.
Just leave it."

"All right, all right," she says,

while I'm thinking
*Don't ask about Benjamin.*

I don't want her interfering.
I want to keep it for me.

"So," she says.
"Benjamin Jones?
Would you?"

"No," I say quickly.

Then Harriet
wrinkles her nose and goes,
"Well, I think he's into *you.*
Do you want me to help you?"

"No!" I say.

"He's pretty hot,
don't you think?"

"Sure," I say.
#Understatement.
But I can't help
smiling as I think
about him.

Harriet looks at me,
then stops and

cocks her head and says,
"You look so pretty.
Smile like that again.
I'll take a picture of you."

So I do.

# Gossip

Dad picks Harriet and me up
behind the skating rink
at five past twelve,
like he promised.

"Very cloak-and-dagger,"
he says as I get in the front seat.
                    I have no idea what he means.
                    Nothing new there.

Harriet tries to get in the back,
but it's covered in Dad's cycling crap.

"Sorry!" he says, reaching behind
and shoving his stuff out of the way,
"I've been mountain biking today."

"Cool, where did you go?" Harriet asks,
like an enormous suck-up,
giving Dad the cue to go into
way more detail than
anyone wanted him to.

Finally Dad asks me, "How was work?
Did you ask about the form
for the internship?"

                    "Mmm-hmm," I say.

"What's that?" Harriet says.

"Oh, just that summer thing
at the planetarium.
It's kind of nerdy."

"Ooh, will you get one for me?
I've always thought
it sounded cool," she says,
more to Dad than me.

"You can just apply online," I say.
"I only picked a form up
because I was there today.
It's a ton of work, you know.
You have to get a reference
from someone in astronomy.
And you need to be free
all summer."

"Imagine if we both got it!
It could be amazing.
You and me! Doing astronomy!"

"Yeah," I say, glancing
at Harriet in the back.
"That would be amazing."

"So, what about your night, girls?"
says Dad. "Anyone *make out*?"

"Dad!" I groan.

"What?" he says. "I just want
a little gossip. Consider it my fare.
Come on . . . who made out with who?"

"Uh. No one calls it
'making out' anymore," I say.

"What do they call it?"

"*They* don't call it anything.
And *you* don't talk about it.
Don't even think about it.
We'd rather give you *money*
than gossip."

We're waiting
at a red light
when Harriet leans
into the middle,

and I glance at her face
glowing red
in the reflected light

all confessional,
and says,
   "I didn't make out with anyone,
   but Jackson did ask
   if he could DM me."

"Gossip!" Dad squeals, clapping,
like he thinks he's one of us.
"You have always been
my favorite, Harry."

"Traitor," I mutter.
Harriet ignores me.

# The Tree House

Harriet's and my telescope
lives in the tree house
between our yards,
where we used to

  have tea parties
      and make mud pies
            and rose perfume
            out of decomposing petals
            and mulchy leaves.

Now when we use it
we stay up late, talking
      and stargazing
            and taking photos of
            stars and
            planets and
            the moon.

Then we sneak to the bakery
to get the first pastries,
before finally going
to sleep at dawn.

I'm exhausted from
standing up, talking all day,
but Harriet wants
to go to the tree house tonight,
and our parents say it's OK.

I move the telescope
to the waxing crescent moon:
a perfect sliver of possibility.

"It's clear," I say to Harriet.
"You should come and see."

But Harriet lies
on her back,
dangling her legs
over the edge,
making the canopy rustle
in the night breeze.

"I'm busy," she sighs,
her eyes on her phone,

missing the stars
shining bright
right above us.

# Top Three

"Busy doing what?"

"Thinking about
*Mr. Number One,*"
she says,
rolling onto her tummy
to face me.

Me and Harriet always
play Top Three.

The top three things we're
thinking about,
or worrying about,
or obsessing about,

on any given week,
or night,
or hour.

Harriet's top three recently?
Boys, boys, boys.

"OK, then.
Who is he?"

"Actually,
there's a new entry . . ."
She sits up,
pulls her knees into her belly,

and performs a drumroll
on the floorboards
with her feet.
"At number one . . .
Elon Musk."

"Ew!" I say.
"Elon Musk is not hot."

"Yes, he is. He is so hot.
And really smart.
I'm talking
major
      cooch

         quivers."

(*Ugh.*)

"I've been reading
everything I can
about space travel."

"And me, for my application,"
I say, then immediately regret
mentioning it.

"Ooh! What do we have
to do for it again?"

"Write a long essay.
And get a glowing reference
from someone with evidence
of your passion for astronomy."

I know I'm making it sound hard.
"I was thinking of asking Mr. B
to write one for me.
And to check my application."

"Oh, Mr. B!
He's still top three."

"Please, Harry.
We've talked about this.
He's too old!
And he's a *teacher*."

"Hey! No judgment,
remember?"

"OK. Sorry.
Go on, then.
Let's have it.
Top three."

She puts down her phone
for a moment,
using her fingers
to check off her crushes.

"One: Elon Musk.
Two: probably still Lee,
Three: Mr. B . . .
            and his thighs."

Harriet lies back again,
picks up her phone,
and sighs.

"His *thighs*?" I say.
"WTF?"

"Shh," she says, jabbing me.
"You're interrupting my fantasy.
He was covering PE on Friday.
Tiny shorts.

His thighs are
                unbelievably
                        meaty."

                "MEATY?" I shout.
                        Then gag.
                "Don't say 'meaty.'"

"Mmm," she says, sighing,
rubbing her thighs,
"meaty meaty meaty."

                "What was he doing
                        covering PE?"

"I think he was subbing,"
she says to her phone.
"I'd sub for him any day."

                "What does that even mean?"

"No idea . . ."
she says, giggling,
lifting her head up
and twisting to look at me.

"But he *is* dreamy."
She grins, then she
lies back again,

                    and I look down at her,
                    with her legs swinging
                    into the cool evening,
                    stirring up the oily
                    scent of the tree.

                    "What about Jackson?"
                    I ask, to get away
        from thinking about Mr. B
                    in tiny shorts
                    and to stop her saying
                    the *m*-word again.
                    "Do you like him?"

"Kind of,"
she says, shrugging.
"We're messaging right now.
Should I send him this?"
She turns her phone
to show me
a pouty,
booby
selfie.

                    "Oh my god!" I scream.
                    "You are crazy."

"What's the big deal?" she says.
"Come on, he's asking me
for a selfie."

"He'll show *everyone*.
Like he did with those girls."

"I'm only showing a little bra.
You know, you can be
such a nun."

"Only compared to you," I say.
"You've got the hots
for everyone."

"And you for no one."

I think about mentioning
Benjamin,
but she's still focused on
her selfie anyway.

"Maybe I won't send it.
It's not that flattering.
What do you really think?"

"Don't send it," I snap.
"Don't be so nuts."

"You're no fun anymore!" she says,
and slaps her phone down
and flips over to look at me.

"What about you, O queen
of the parched vag?
What's your top three?"

*Benjamin,*
*Benjamin,*
*Benjamin,*
I think.

But I say,
"My essay,
my reference,
and whether we'll get
that picture of
the blood moon
in a couple of weeks."

"Oh, yeah, the blood moon!"
she says, clapping her hands,

surprising me that she's
still excited about our
joint love of
astronomy
and photography.

I feel a bit bad that
I thought she wasn't
interested in anything
except boys.

"I've been researching
what we should do with
this blood moon.
I have tons of ideas
we can try."
She gets out her phone

to show me.
"See this one," she says.
"Wouldn't the silhouette
of the tree look amazing?"

"Totally," I say.
"I just hope
the sky is clear.
The forecast is really bad."

"Don't worry," she says.
"I just know it'll be
the perfect night."

I love how Harriet's
always so positive.
"I hope you're right."

"I'm *always* right."
She grins. "Now,
back to boys,
tell me who you like.
Is it Benjamin?"

"No," I say,
a bit too quickly.

"Come on, I'm bored.
Give me something juicy."

"I have nothing juicy," I say.
"Although, maybe there's
something you can tell me . . ."

"Anything."

"OK . . . so say I *did*
like somebody . . .
Hypothetically.
How would I know
what to do,
you know if I ended
up *with them*,
intimately?"

Harriet snorts. "Intimately,"
she says, doing an all-too-accurate
impression of me.

Then she breathes out dreamily.
"Don't worry," she says, sighing.
"When you're with someone
you really like
you just *k n o w* what to do."

"I believe
that's true for you.
You're always so relaxed talking
to somebody you like.
But you're so much more
confident than me."

"I'm not really," she says,
and for a moment she looks
small and weak.
Then she rolls back her shoulders
and pushes her chest out at me.

"I'm just faking it
until I start making it."
She pouts and waggles her
eyebrows at me.

"What does *that* even mean?"

"I don't know,"
she says, giggling,
then she gets up
and moves over
to the telescope.

"OK, let me have a look,"
she says, nudging me.
"And Frankie,"
she adds, putting her face
to the eyepiece,
"if you do like someone,
just be yourself.
Yourself is great."

# Little Lies

On Sunday morning,
Harriet messages me
asking if she can use my printer,
under the pretense that mine is better
because you can print almost anything on it,
including something
she says she needs for her French project,
but I know she wants to
      do homework
      together.

I'd rather do it
      on my own,
because lately,
Harriet is always
distracting me
or copying me,
or talking about
the latest boy
she likes.

I tell her she can use it later
because I'm going
to help Mom with work
at her school's lab,
and instead
I slip out of the house

and go down to the library
to work alone.

And while I work
I think about the possibility
of Benjamin
popping in to get something
and coming over to talk to me.
Or sitting opposite me,
and us doing our
homework together
and talking
passionately
about physics and stuff
because Benjamin
is sciencey like me.
Or maybe us
ending up
in between two quiet shelves . . .
kissing or something.
#Hypocrisy

# Dress Code

Harriet opens her front door
wearing a low-cut T-shirt,
reeking of perfume,
and with so much makeup on
I wonder for a second
if it's Saturday,
not Monday.

"You're not going to school
like that, are you?" I ask
before I can stop myself.

"Good morning to you too,"
she says, rolling her eyes.
"I can wear what I like.
Anyway, it's the *natural look*."

"RuPaul style.

You're going to
get into trouble."
Why does she have to
be so reckless?

I wonder whether she's
dressed like this for Mr. B.

I still can't believe
she likes him.

"For what?
Wearing a T-shirt?
Come off it.
Still rocking the nun vibe
I see," she says, taking in
my skinny jeans
and retro NASA hoodie,

which I was hoping
made me look clever,
rather than nunny.

"If nuns can be astronomers,
then sure," I say, laughing it off,
but wishing I'd worn
just a bit of makeup.
I wonder if I'll see
Benjamin today.

Just then, Harriet's mom
comes out of their kitchen,
drinking a green smoothie,
her slinky bathrobe
sliding over
her bare legs.

"Bye, girls," she calls
as she heads upstairs.
"Give 'em hell."

# Distractions

Our class is gathered
for assembly
in the auditorium,
with the principal.

The audience lights are
on, and Mr. Adamson
is going on and on
about (the girls')
dress code.
#We'veHeardThisOne

"We must eliminate distractions
to your education.
Exams are soon.
I don't want anyone failing.
   I don't want to see
         short skirts . . ."

                              (he says this to
                                    three girls
                              in the front row)
            "hair dye . . ."

                              (at Bethany,
                        who has dyed hers
                              bright blue)
                  "or inappropriate makeup."
                              (at Harriet)

"They are all distracting."

"For who?" Harriet hisses in my ear.
"Him? The crusty old perv."

                                    I wish she'd stop
                                  drawing attention
                                        to herself,
                         but she does have a point.
                                   I'm not sure who
                            is going to find it hard
                           to concentrate in class
                           because of Bethany's
                                 cobalt-blue bob.

                              And if anyone does,
                             I can't help thinking
                               that's their problem.

                         I glance around the room,
                   wondering where Benjamin
                          usually sits in assembly.

                              When it's almost over,
                                          I spot him,
                                         a few rows
                                      in front of me.

                              He doesn't see me.

# Shameless

Mr. Adamson pushes past us
as we leave assembly,
"Excuse me, ladies."

"Sorry, sir," I say,
moving out of his way.

Harriet flutters her lashes
at his back and says,
"I hope I don't make anyone
think about anything
*uneducational* today."

"Stop!" I hiss.
She's so reckless.

"What?" she says.
"That jerk has the nerve
to suggest that my makeup
might make someone fail
their exams.
I'm not OK with it."

"You are shameless."

"And you're a coward.
You hate him
as much as I do.
Don't pretend
you respect him.

"Sorry, sir!" she says,
doing a mean impression of me.

Then she trots off
to catch up with Leylah
and Bethany, saying,
"Did your dad go insane
about your hair?"

But before they're too far away,
she turns around, hands in prayer,
and says, "See you in physics,
Sister Frankie."

# Changes

Me and Harriet
have been besties
since I can remember.

I know when
we were in second grade
in Mr. Parlow's class
literally *everything*
was funny to us.

I wish we could go back
to being silly all the time,
but the feeling of it,
the freeness of it,
is gone.

I wish Harriet would stop
reminding me
I'm not as fun as I
used to be.

Although, now I wonder
if I was ever as free
as she seems to be.

# Chances

Harriet wants us to sit at the front
of the physics lab,
probably so that Mr. B
can see her smoky eyes,

but it suits me
because I want to know
if he got my email asking him
to write a reference for me.

"Today, we're looking at
weight and mass," he says.
"Settle down now,
let gravity guide you
to your seats, ha ha."

Harriet laughs really loudly.

                              All through class,
                              I scribble madly,
                        taking in every word
                              he says

while Harriet drops her pen
every five minutes,
and struts to get it,
bending over
            o u t r a g e o u s l y   s l o w l y
right in front of Mr. B.

After class I linger

wanting to ask
about the reference
on my own,
but Mr B comes over to me.

"I'll write your reference
and give it to you Friday.
Do you want me to
read your application too?"

                              "Yes, please," I say.

"I think you have
a really good chance,"
he says.

I feel my face flush
with pride that he has recognized
this is *my* special thing.

                              "I'll email it later,
                              if that's okay," I say,
                              picking up my bag.

"Absolutely," Mr. B says.
"Nice hoodie, by the way,"
he adds as I go through
the doorway.

Behind me I hear Harriet say,
"Can you look at mine too, sir?"

"Of course," says Mr. B.
But then he says,

"You have it now?
OK, stay behind.
I'll take a look at it
right away."

I hear her say
"I just love the stars . . ."
but I have to move to let
the rest of the class
file out.

So it's from outside
that I watch her
lean over his desk

                              (so inappropriately)

while he reads
her application

                              before mine.

# We'd Be All Right

No chance of stars,
it's raining,
but even so
Harriet and I
go up to
the tree house
after dark.

> "So, did Mr. B
> like your application?" I ask,
> while she gets her laptop
> out of her backpack.

"Yeah," she says vaguely.

> "What did he say?" I ask,
> wondering if
> he thinks she's got a
> *really good chance.*

"Oh, you know."

> "No," I say. "What?
> Did he read the essay?
> Did he suggest any changes?
> Did he think it was a good topic?"

"Frankie, can we
just leave it?"

"Sorry," I say.
If it was me
I'd want to talk about
it all evening.
"I was just asking."

Harriet scowls at me.
"Look, we're not all
Mr. B's favorite,
you massive physics nerd,
so it wasn't exactly a shower
of glory. And I don't feel
like talking about it.
Especially to you."

"I'm sure it's great,"
I say, trying to sound
encouraging
but realizing I probably sound
patronizing.

She's on her phone,
so I set up the laptop,
then wait for her

as she laughs
then sighs and frowns.

"What's up?" I ask lightly,
hoping we can
change the tone.

"It's Jackson," she says.
"He won't stop messaging."

"I thought you liked him."

"I did," she says. "But now
it's getting kind of boring."

"I told you not
to get involved."

"No, you didn't.
And now he's obsessed.
And you know how
he told us he got with
those two girls that night?
They're his cousins!"

I burst out laughing.
"That's incest."

Harriet whacks me.
"Obviously nothing happened.
He lied to brag.
I'm not into that,
know what I mean?"

"Totally," I say.
But I want to stop talking
about Jackson and get on
with our evening.

"How do I get rid of him?"

"Tell him you don't like him?"

"Ooh," she says, typing,

"I'll tell him I'm busy
and I'm in love with someone else."

                    "Harry," I say. "That's lying!
                              Just tell the truth.
                         And then can we please
                    watch *The Walking Dead*?"

"Absolutely," she says,
hitting send
and then turning it
to show me.

She's written
that she's *with me* with me
and not to contact her again
because of my jealousy.

                         "Harry!" I say.
                    "You're ridiculous."

"It's fine," she says.
"Everyone lies a bit.
He'll know what it means.
I'm saving him face."

                              I'm just glad
                    she's not taking things
                    any further with him.

She tucks her phone away
and pulls the snacks out
of her backpack,

then reaches over to the laptop
and presses play.

We nestle into the pile of pillows
and with the fairy lights twinkling,
and us alternating eating
tortilla chips and tangerines,
we spend the evening
scream-laughing at the
incompetence of everyone
        except Rick Grimes.

                            (Actual cooch quivers.)

"You're drooling!"

                                        "Am not."

"You can't have the hots
for Rick, and tell me
Mr. B is old."

                                    "Different rules
                                for the apocalypse."

"Stab it!"
Harriet shouts.
"You idiot."

                            "Shut the door!" I yell.

"Use the machete!"
Harriet screams.

*"Run away!"* I say.

"Use the machine guns!"
Harriet says.

"Lock the doors and hide!"
I say, feeling safe

up here, in our tree house,
where no one can get us,

watching other people
being clueless,
and knowing, if it was us,

we'd be all right.

Well, actually,
I'd be scared shitless.

But Harriet
is actually pretty brave.

# Lunchtime

In the dining hall
I sit with Leylah and Bethany
and subtly scan the room
for Benjamin.
I start to eat
my saucy spaghetti
(carefully)
(in case Benjamin's watching me).

Harriet sits down heavily
and sips her large
black coffee.
"Ugh." She shudders,
swallowing, grimacing.
"This is so bitter.
It's disgusting."

"Why are you drinking it, then?"
asks Leylah, laughing,
opening a can
of soda.

"Because I'm dying," Harriet says.
"I didn't go to sleep until four a.m."

"Sexting Jackson?"
says Bethany, nudging Harriet.

"I told you," she says,
leaning away from Bethany,
"I ended it with him.
And your lunch
absolutely stinks."

"All right," says Bethany.
"Don't take it out on me."

"I'm sorry," says Harriet,
running her hands over her face
and groaning. "I'm just so tired."

        "What were you even doing?"
        I ask. "I was with you
        until about ten."

"I was rewriting
my application to
send to Mr. B."

        "Oh," I say.
        I feel a pang of jealousy.
        What if hers was
        better than mine?
        "Did you get it done?"

"Barely," she says. "I sent it
this morning, then had
about two hours' sleep.
But I think I made
a horrible mistake."
Harriet groans

and folds her body forward,
resting her forehead
on the table.

Marie says,
"Nothing good gets done
after ten p.m., if you ask me."

"Well, I didn't," Harriet says
from under her hair.

"I'm sure it's not as bad
as you're imagining,"
says Leylah.

"What if it's worse?"
Harriet mumbles.

I try to think of
something reassuring
to say, but just then

I see Benjamin
walking toward me
and I'm briefly distracted
wiping my face
and smiling at him.

He grins at me
as he walks past me.
God, he's dreamy.

When I look back,
Bethany is patting Harriet's head.

"I'm sure it's great."

"You'll feel better
after a good night's rest,"
says Marie.

"Enough with the sleep, Marie,"
Harriet moans.
"And Beth," she adds,
"you had better
not be getting
tuna in my hair.
It took me an hour
this morning."

And we all giggle
as Bethany licks
her fingers
quickly
before resuming her patting.

# Extraction

That afternoon, in history,
a freshman
knocks on the open door,
with a piece of paper
trembling in her hand.
"I have a message
from Mr. Adamson."

Ms. Wyse
beckons the girl,
lowers her glasses,
reads the note,
and sighs.
"Harriet Prosser,
he wants to see you."

Harriet glances at me.
She looks worried.
Then she gets up
and quietly slips
out the door,
and as I hear her footsteps
fade down the hall
my stomach knots.

What's she done?

# Distractions

Mr. Adamson lectured us about distractions
for about an hour just
yesterday.

I can't think of many things more distracting
than extracting someone in the middle of class
with no explanation.

Apparently Mr. Adamson's
second lesson of the week is
irony.

# Speculation

After Harriet leaves
we're supposed to be reading in silence,
but everyone is whispering
and the boys are all giggling.
I can hear
from the buzzing
that something
is going around.

I remember once,
when Mohammed's mom had a baby,
he got to leave early.

Another time Caylee's grandmother
was in the hospital, dying,
and she got called out of class.
Apparently she only just made it
in time to say goodbye.

Births and deaths.
What could be dramatic enough
to warrant Harriet's extraction?

Everyone has a theory,
but I know it's about
what she mentioned at lunch.
The "horrible mistake."

Then between classes
in the hall I hear Harriet's

name and see
Jackson, Dev, and Charlie,
laughing and whooping,
their necks craning
around Harriet's phone!
They're taking pictures
with their phones
of her screen.

I push myself
in to see an email
Harriet has sent.

To Mr. B.

                    I grab her phone from the boys.
                        "You can't just take
                    things out of people's bags!"

"It fell out," says Jackson,
holding his hands up.
"I was just looking after it."

                        "Bullshit," I say.
                    "How did you open it?"

"Passcode 0, 0, 0, 0.
It's pretty easy to see it
when you sit behind somebody
and you know
they love Oreos."
He snorts, looking between
Dev and Charlie, adding,
"Easy. Ha. Just like her."

God, he's disgusting.
"You better not have
done anything,"
I say, turning away

and leaving them
whooping and
calling after me
to lighten up.
Down the corridor
I look at her screen
and read

the email.

She's sent him her
application again,
and attached a selfie.

She's in bed, wearing
a low-cut pajama top
and she's leaning in,
her boobs squeezed.
She's written:
"Hopefully you'll agree
I've worked really hard on this.
Can you check it over again?"

Ugh, Harriet.
I cannot believe her.
Does she ever think
about the consequences
before doing something?

# Trouble

I sit in geography,
worrying.
Harriet's going to be
in so much trouble.
You can't send a picture
like that to a teacher
and get away with it.
What was she thinking?

                 I check my phone
       under the desk for news,
        unable to concentrate
          and wondering
        what's happening
           to her now.

Mr. B must have told the principal.
They might suspend her.
What if they expel her?

I don't know whether to cry
or scream.

                    Then
        an unknown number
         messages me.

In detention. Meet me
in the bathroom in ten.
H

I wait in geography
for nine minutes,
feeling sick, finding it
impossible to concentrate
on anything Ms. Allison says,
which is annoying because
she told us
our next test
will be on
this tectonic activity.

Finally it's time.
I slip Harriet's phone
out of my backpack
and into my pocket
next to mine.
I go to the front,
ask for a pass
to go to the bathroom.

Ms. Allison
looks at me
suspiciously.
"Quickly, then,"
she says, like she knows
I'm up to something.
"Five minutes,
or I'll come check on you."

# Fight

I hurry down
the silent hallway,
Ms. Allison's words
repeating in my head.
"Five minutes," she said.
If she checks up on me
they'll find Harry too.
(Meeting someone
while skipping detention
got Joseph Carlton
a monthlong suspension.)

The bathroom door
bangs shut behind me,
making me jump.
I'm so worried
I'm already sweating.

"Harriet?" I whisper,
peering around
stall doors.

A hollow sniff echoes
from the last stall.

Harriet's perched on
the toilet seat,
streaks of black mascara
on her cheeks.

Once in elementary school
Harriet hid in the bathroom
because Lena Kowalski
said her head was too small,
and we ended up laughing
about it.

I don't know if laughter
can help us now.

I crouch down next to her,
hug her,
squeeze her
trembling body.
"Oh, Harry," I say.

What else can I say?

"Frankie," she says, sobbing,
practically hyperventilating.
"I'm in so much trouble."

"Why are you out of detention,
and whose phone did you
text me from?" I ask her,
checking over my shoulder,
hoping nobody else comes in.

But she's crying so much,
I can't understand
what she's saying,
and her sobs are echoing
all around the bathroom.

"Shh," I say, ripping off some toilet paper,
checking the time as I wind
the paper around my hand.
I've already been gone
two minutes.

"Just breathe," I tell her.

Harriet sits up and
blows her nose
then drops the soggy
wad into the toilet
between her legs and
takes a deep breath.

I sweep my thumbs
under her eyes
to dry her tears
and clean her face.

"Don't judge me,
Frankie," she says.
"But I sent something
I shouldn't have."

"I know," I say. "I've already seen."
I take her phone from my pocket
and put it on her knee.
"Jackson had it.
He saw your passcode
over your shoulder.
They got a copy.
I'm really sorry."

"Ugh," she moans.
"So embarrassing.
And Mr. Adamson gave
me such a lecture.
He says I'm getting
detention all week."

        "Well, that's not surprising."
Harriet looks up and
narrows her eyes at me.

           "Sorry," I say.
      "What are you going to do?"

"I was thinking . . . maybe
I can say I didn't send it?"

        "Or you could take some
       responsibility?" I let out
      before I can stop myself.

"Thanks, Frankie," she says.

         "All right," I say,
     holding my hands up.
      "I just don't think
    you should start lying."

"I can't believe Mr. B told on me!
Mr. Adamson said
the photo might be classed
as *child pornography*."

        "Oh my god! Harry!

Do you not think
that's *why* he told on you?"

"Calm down, Frankie,"
Harriet says flippantly.
"It's just a tiny bit of boob.
There's no way Mr. Adamson
will call the police.
He's exaggerating
to scare me."

I check the time,
I've been gone four
minutes.
#ShitShitShit
"It's not *just boob*.
Don't you get it?
This is serious.
What is Mr. B going to
think of me?"

"What does it have
to do with you?"

"Everything!" I shout,
forgetting to whisper.
"I'm your best friend.
He knows we're
always together.
He's going to think
I endorsed it!"

"Oh my god," she says.
"'Endorsed it'. . .

Get over yourself!"

"Me? What's your problem lately?
You need to
take this seriously!"

Harriet's tears have stopped.
She stares at me coldly.
Her mascara is gone,
her foundation too.
Her freckles are showing
like they always used to
when we were little
before she wore makeup

only I don't recognize
who she is anymore.

"I *am* taking it seriously,"
she says.
"Why do you think
I was so depressed at lunch?
I know it was stupid."

"You're not taking
anything seriously.
You're all over the place,
chasing Lee,
texting Jackson."

I have less than one
minute to get back to class
before Ms. Allison comes in.

"And now sending Mr. B

that slutty selfie!"

"*Slutty?*" she screams.
"Fucking hell, Frankie!
You think you're
soooo
PERFECT!"

"Harriet!" I snap. "Shut up!
Or we'll both get busted."

"Oh, and if *Saint Frankie* got
into trouble, *that* would be
the end of the world."

"Hey," I say. "That is *not fair*.
I don't want to be here."

"Then don't be," she shouts,
shoving past me.
"You're not helping me.
You're just judging me!"

I reach out to stop her,
but she flings me
off her

so violently
I slip on the tiles
and fall to the floor.

I stare at her,
pain exploding
in my hip where I landed,
and in that moment

I hate every bone
in her body.

She spins around
and looks at me
and I see in her eyes
that she also hates me.

She moves and I think
she's going to hit me.
"I am
            done with you,"
                        she yells.
"You're NOTHING TO ME!"

                        "Good!" I shout.
                        "I don't want to be
                                    friends with
                        a slut anyway!"

Then she storms to the door,
opens it, and shouts
into the corridor,
"FRANKIE YOUNG IS
SKIPPING CLASS.
BUT I MADE HER DO IT."

She looks down
at me on the floor
and whispers,
"Happy now?"
then whips her hair
over her shoulder
and struts out.

# Happy?

I'm terrified
a teacher
heard and I might
get detention,
or worse.

I'm furious
she deliberately
tried to get me
into trouble.

I'm hurting
where I fell
when she
pushed me.

I'm worried
Harriet might
get into trouble
with the police,
or Mr. B might
lose his job.

I'm frustrated
with Harriet
for not taking
anything seriously.

And I'm aching
inside more

than I could
ever have imagined
that she said
"You're nothing to me."

Those words
echo inside me,
making me feel empty.

*Nothing to me.*
*Nothing to me.*
*Nothing to me.*

# Later

Harriet isn't
out front
after school.

I walk home,
alone,
seething,

and even though
she shouted at me
that I'm nothing to her

I'm still not quite
angry enough
not to miss her,
just slightly.

# Talking

That evening,
I try not to look at my phone.
Harriet can deal with
this on her own.

> She doesn't want me.
> She said I'm nothing
> to her anyway.

I go to the living room,
with a heavy feeling
and a stomachache,
to half watch *The Great British Baking Show*
with Mom and Dad,
with my physics textbook
on my lap.

"Are you OK?" asks Mom,
looking up from
a pile of grading.

> "No," I say.
> "I hate everyone
> and everything."

"PMS?" says Mom.

> "Maybe," I reply
> gloomily.

"Cuddle?" says Dad.
"You're not doing homework.
You haven't turned the page
for about three cakes."

"No, thanks," I say,
ignoring Dad's hurt face.
"Me and Harriet had a fight."

"Have you tried talking about it?"
Mom says, taking off her glasses.

"Ugh," I say.
"We're way
past talking."

"You said that last time."
Dad mutes the TV,
swings his legs around
so he's facing me
then crosses them and leans toward me
"Come on, talk to *us*."

"No," I say.
"I don't want you
to be all reasonable
and understanding.
She's a bitch."

"Language," says Mom,
putting her grading aside.

But Dad pouts sassily,
then flicks his nonexistent

hair over his shoulder
and squeals,
"Tell me she did not make out with
that boy I like?
I'll *kill* her if she even
looks at him
one
more
time!"

"Arggh, Dad! Stop it.
And I told you,
no one says
*make out* anymore."

"Swap saliva?" he says.
"Smooch?
French ki—"

"Dad!"

"Come on, Frankie,"
says Mom, tucking her
hair behind her ears.
"What did Harry do?"

I shake my head.
I can't tell them.

It's too embarrassing.
What if they think
that's the kind of thing
we're all doing?

"Well, we're always here
if you want to talk," says Mom,
putting her glasses back on.

Dad starts to sing the chorus
to "You've Got a Friend."

                              "DAD!" I shout,

but Mom gives him a
serious look over the top
of her glasses and he stops,
acting out zipping his lips.

                    "Thank you," I say to her.

"At your service," says Mom,
going back to her grading.

"But you should talk about it,"
she says, without looking up.
"Talking always makes it better.
Sometimes worse first.
But always better."

                         "Yeah, yeah," I say.
                         I've heard it before.

"Listen to your mother,"
Dad mumbles
out the side
of his mouth,
"She is very wise."
Then he unmutes the TV.

# Explosion

When I go up to bed
and I'm finally alone
I can't help checking my phone.
PEANUT BUTTER AND JELLY
has exploded:
A hundred and
fifty-eight messages.

Harriet's whining
because the whole
school knows she
basically sexted Mr. B.

I only skim-read.

The girls all share screenshots of
what everyone's saying
in other groups
so that Harriet can see
and they can help
her be outraged
about Mr. B telling on her.

(Instead of addressing
the real problem,
which is Harriet
not taking responsibility
for her own stupidity.)

And then I see

they're all saying
they've seen the picture
and they don't think
she's a *slut*.


My stomach sinks.
My insides shrink.

She's turned
them against me.
She told them
about our fight
and what I said
and they've decided
Harriet's right.
#TakingSides


I go to the bathroom
to brush my teeth
and through the cracked
open window
I can hear Harriet crying.

When we were little
we used to do bird calls
through these exact windows
late at night
if we wanted to talk.

We'd sit on the sills
and chat until
one of our parents
caught us and told us
it was time to go to sleep.

I listen to Harriet weep.
I'm so
angry with her
for shouting at me,
pushing me,
for trying to get me
into trouble today,
for saying
"You're nothing to me,"
that
I cannot say
~~that I care about her~~
~~that I don't want her to be hurt~~
~~that she's **everything** to me~~
~~how she's my best friend~~
~~and I love her~~
anything.

I close the bathroom
door behind me,
and get into bed,
and pull the covers
up around me,
salty anger spilling
onto my sheets.

It takes me
ages to get to sleep.

# Thighs

I can't remember when
I last walked to school
without Harriet.
We've walked together
since we were ten
and before that
literally every day
with my dad on his way
to work at the bike shop.

Sometimes he used to
let us take turns
sitting on the seat and
he'd wheel us along,
deliberately wobbling
with us giggling.

I slip out quickly,
avoiding Mom, and I
go the long way so I don't
have to pass Harriet's house.
There's no way
we're walking together today.
I don't want to even see her.

The going is slow
without any gossip.

I've only walked down
three streets and already it feels
like it's taking an eternity.

But as I turn down
the next street,
I see Benjamin,
closing his front gate.

He must have been
walking this way
since we were in
elementary school,
but I never knew.

He's so hot.
(And so cool.)

I push thoughts of
Harriet aside, and
pull myself up tall,
set my eyes
to the parting clouds,
like I'm deep in thought,
perhaps about the way
the morning sun creates
crepuscular rays.

"Frankie!" he says,
with a nod.

"Hey, Benjamin!" I say.
"I didn't know you lived here."
(Which is perfectly true,

except now that I do,
I'm always coming this way.)

Benjamin has a sports bag
slung over his shoulder,

and I don't know
what else to say,
so I ask,
"Have you got PE today?"

"Rugby tryouts," he says.
"School team. Lunchtime."

"Cool," I say.
"But aren't you already
on the team?"

"Yeah," he says. "But
these are tryouts for the
starting lineup."

"What position
do you play?"

"Second row.
You're supposed to be tall
and strong.
I've got the height,
but I need to work
on my upper back.
My lats, you know."

"No," I say.

"What part is that?"

"Here." He pats the muscles
beneath his armpits.
"I'm supposed to be training.
Doing weights, you know?
Or, like, giving piggybacks.

If you need a ride . . . ?"
he offers me his back,
but

                    I cannot reply.
              My tongue is suddenly
              too big for my mouth.

              We walk a few steps
                    in silence,
            and I wonder if he's
           imagining the same
                 thing as me.

           Me jumping on him,
           our bodies touching,
          and me *riding him*.

I glance at him, and
Benjamin
is
blushing.

             My cheeks go red
        and I feel myself getting

hot
hot
hot.

I look down,
searching for
something to say,
but Benjamin's legs
are in my eyes' way.
His jeans *cling*
to his rugby-tight thighs
and all at once
I realize
the power
of a meaty pair of thighs.

I wonder what it
would be like
to bite them

and at the same time
I wonder what it
would be like
to tell Benjamin
this is what I'm thinking.

It's hard to imagine
doing something
so outrageous.

"I had so much fun
on Saturday,"

he says. "I was hoping to
see you Monday,
or yesterday."

"Me too," I say.

"I really liked
hanging out with you."

I giggle, though
I don't mean to.

"Hey," he says, stopping
next to the park railings.
"Don't laugh at me.
I'm trying to say
I'm into you."

I stop too, though
it's hard to not move
because suddenly
I'm full of rocket fuel.

"I like you too," I say,
easily,
feeling my volatile
insides ignite.
"It was too bad
that night ended
when it did."

I take a step closer.

And Benjamin draws
a little nearer to me
and says, "Do you think
it's too early?"

"For what?" I ask,
so close I can feel
the toasty warmth
of his breath on my face
and realize that he's
talking
about
kissing.

"For this," he says,
then leans in
and brings his lips
close to mine

and I move my lips
closer to his,
and just like that
we're

kissing
by the fence
in the golden
bright
morning
sunshine.

#Amazing

# Cold Shoulders and Piggybacks

In *The Walking Dead*
the zombies are always
biting people's necks.
But as I leave Benjamin
at the school gate,
I glance again
at his thighs
and realize if there is
an instinctive part
of the human brain
dedicated to eating
human flesh
it would definitely make
zombies bite the thighs.

They are,
undeniably,
the *meatiest* part
of the human body.

I stifle a snort
as I catch up with Marie,
and we walk into
physics class.
I wish Harriet were here.
Marie wouldn't get
why that's funny.

But then I realize
that Marie
hasn't actually said
a word to me.

I guess Harriet did
a thorough job
of turning her
against me.

I look around to get
one more glimpse of
Benjamin, and instead
see Harriet get out of
her mom's bright yellow car
and walk through the gates,
head held high.

We file inside the physics lab,
and Marie very deliberately
doesn't sit next to me.
She takes the last seat
in the row behind
where we usually sit
with Harriet.

Then the room comes alive
with whispers and murmurs,
and a classroom of heads follow
as Harriet approaches.

She flicks her hair
theatrically for the benefit
of everyone watching.

I can't believe she's
enjoying this moment.
She looks totally fine.
Happy even.
I guess Mr. Adamson
didn't call the police.

~~I wish he would.~~
~~She deserves it.~~

Harriet is heading toward
our classroom door, but then
she goes right past,
and I watch through the window
as she goes into
the other class.

I guess Harriet got moved
so Mr. B isn't teaching her.
I sit on my own.
I take out my phone
under the desk
just to check.

We're not allowed
phones in class;
we're supposed to
leave them in our lockers.
Not that anyone does.

But Mr. B won't be
expecting me
to break the rules.

I have a message from
Benjamin.
I open it,
smile at it.
Benjamin's message says,
"Piggyback home?"

I want to say *yes* because
all I can think of are
rugby-tight thighs.
Rugby-tight
**thigh**s.

My finger hovers over reply.
God, I want to . . .
(bite his thighs).
How should I reply?

But while I'm thinking,
I'm not listening
to anything happening
in the room, because
my mind is off with Benjamin.

Then Marie kicks
the back of my chair,
and I look up and hear
Mr. B say, "Ahem,"
in his particular way.

He scowls at me and taps the
box for confiscated phones.

I get up
and drop mine in,
blushing because I
usually wouldn't dare to
be
actually
messaging.

On my way back to my seat,
I smile at Marie,
but she won't look at me.

# Momentum

"Open your books to page
one hundred and twelve,"
says Mr. B. "Momentum."

I copy the equation
he's written on the board:
*momentum = mass x velocity.*

But then I start thinking,
if Benjamin gave me
a piggyback home,
how much more momentum
would we have
than if we were walking alone—
        "Frankie?" says Mr. B.

                        I look up.
                "Yes, sir?" I say
            with desperation,
                hoping he'll
        repeat the question.
But he just points at the board
                and waits,
            and time ticks by
        as I try to calculate
    the answer to the equation.

"How about you, Marie?"
says Mr. B.

"Is it sixty?" she says,
glancing at me.

But just in time,
I get there.
"Actually, it's sixty-nine,"
I say to the class,
and everyone laughs.

(But Mr. B doesn't like
that I can get the answer right
without even listening.)
(And neither does Marie.)

"Concentrate, Frankie"
is all he says.

# After

I wait outside for Marie,
with a dull ache
in my belly,
but she passes me
and ignores me.

> "What's up with you?"
> I ask.

She stops and gives me a filthy look,
like I'm scum of the earth.
"Er . . . Harriet?" she says,
like that's enough.

> "What about her?"
> I ask, wondering if
> anything new
> has happened
> that I don't know.

"Wow. Really?" says Marie.
"Frankie, she's supposed to be,
like, your best friend.
And yesterday she had
*the worst* day,
and when she really needed you,
you were too busy judging her
to listen to her."

> I blink slowly.

So that's Harriet's story?
Nothing about her
trying to get me
into trouble?

"What happened with
Mr. Adamson?" I ask.

"Ask her yourself."

"Marie!" I say. "Just tell me.
I saw her this morning.
Did he call the police?"

Marie sighs and faces me.
"She got detention,
like, every day,
after school.
          And you
          didn't
          even
          message
          last night.
Don't you care
about her?"

"Of course I do."

"You've got a funny way
of showing it."

"I . . . I was . . .
I didn't know
what to say."

"Anything would have been better than nothing."

"They didn't call
the police, though.
That's good."

But Marie just
shakes her head
and walks off.

# The Changing Rooms

Harriet has successfully
spread the word
that we had a fight
and I'm the bad guy.

At lunch I get a sandwich
and eat it behind the trees,
where I can see
the boys' rugby tryouts.

I watch Benjamin('s thighs)
and compose my reply
to his question
about carrying me home.

I try to write something sexy,
but that's Harriet's style,
so in the end,
I just put "OK."

Immediately after tryouts,
he replies to me, saying,
"Great! Meet you at the gate."
I go to PE, feeling
(despite my and Harriet's fight)
happy.

In the locker room
Harriet and the girls ignore me,
and instead they
comb through
Harriet's drama
and how shitty it is
that everyone is sharing
the photo Jackson took of her phone.
It's the talk of the school.
We all know there'll be
something new tomorrow.

But anyway, I don't want to speak.
I'm too excited, wondering
whether Benjamin might
actually try to carry me.

So I just put on my leggings,
T-shirt, and sneakers
in silence, with my
inappropriate thoughts
safely sealed behind my lips.

"Whatever
you're smiling about,"
Harriet says, pushing past me,
"I'm not asking,
so get out of my face."

                              I didn't even know
                              I was smiling.

This thing between
Benjamin and me
is making me feel giddy.

It's like air.
You can't see it,
but it's comprised
of a myriad of
infinitesimally
small particles
of unimaginable
complexity and beauty.

Not even Harriet
being bitchy
bothers me.

In the gym
we form a circle
for warm-up,
Harriet opposite me,
scowling.

And when we play basketball,
I join the opposite team
to guard Harriet.
I'm so bouncy.
I absolutely kill it.

# After Gym

After gym,
I'm sticky
and sweating.

I sniff myself.
I stink and
I'm walking home
with Benjamin.

Hardly anyone ever
has a shower
(they're common showers),
but I decide to do it anyway.

I strip and grab a towel
and, with as much dignity
as I can, say:
"I need a shower today,
so look away."

And to my amazement,
Leylah, Marie, Bethany,
and the others
do what I say.

And I realize that I *can* be
pretty brave.

# Locker Room Talk

While I'm in the shower,
Harriet says, "Wow, she's *brave*."

And Leylah says, "Yeah.
I would never
have a shower at school."

Then Bethany says,
"Me neither. For a start, I can't
wash my hair 'cause of the dye.
But anyway, I hate these parts,
and these parts here."

Leylah says, "You've got
a beautiful body, Beth."

And Beth says,
"Aw, thanks, babe."

"You're so gay, Leylah,"
Harriet chips in.

"And?" says Leylah.

"All right, Ley.
Keep your tits on,"
Harriet says.
"Anyway, I meant Frankie is
brave sending Mr. B
this picture of herself . . ."

she holds up my phone.

I hear the sound
of a message sending

and I'm already running,
slipping on wet tiles
as I hear Marie say,

"HARRY! YOU . . .
DID
     *NOT*
        SEND
           THAT?"

# Betrayal

I grab
my phone
out of her hand.

> Harriet has taken
> a picture of me.
> In the shower.
> **Naked.**

> > "Tell me you did not
> > send this to Mr. B," I say,
> > frantically swiping
> > to find my sent items.
> > I can feel tears coming.

"Calm down," Harriet says.
"Of course I didn't.
I just sent it to the girls.
I'm just playing a joke.
Lighten up, why don't you?"

The girls get out their phones,
and Bethany says,
"We'll all delete it,
won't we?"

Leylah nods and looks shocked.
"It's gone," she says.

"Jesus, Harriet,"
Marie says,
"Get some fucking
boundaries."

                              I delete it,
                    then shove my phone
                 back in the front pocket
                        of my backpack.


"Calm down," says Harriet.
"I'm literally
just joking."

                      As I return to the shower,
                            I feel her eyes
                      like a knife in my back.

# Revenge

I turn off the water.
        Dry myself.
                Pull on my clothes.
                        Take deep breaths.
There is total silence.
No one knows
what to say.

And I know
it's a low blow,
but I really want to
get Harriet back.

My mind goes to the
Silent Ladies' Agreement
to NOT bring up how
in elementary school,
second grade,
Harriet pooped
in the middle of assembly.
She's crossed a line.
I will too.

I shake out my wet hair,
then pause in front of her.
"See ya later,
Harriet Pooper."

The others gasp,
but they also laugh.

And that's good enough
for me.

I leave the locker room,
stepping outside,
my still-damp skin
tingling in the wind,

feeling
like
a warrior,

to meet Benjamin.

# Nightclub Thighs

On my way to Benjamin,
Mrs. Lovelie, who teaches health
(and is not at all lovely),
shouts across the field at me.

"Frankie Young!
Roll your skirt down!
You're on the school grounds,
not a nightclub stage!"

Then she walks out the gates,
right past Benjamin,
who is still wearing his
tiny little
rugby shorts
over his
rugby-tight thighs.

*His* are the legs
that should be
on a stage.

# Biology

Benjamin is leaning
against the school wall.
I watch his shoulders rise and fall
as though the air inside him
is riding him
from within.

The early spring wind
sweeps the clouds aside,
and in the sudden sun
his white rugby shirt glows bright.
I blink against his blinding light.

I step a little closer,
my arm muscles stiffening
with a nervously tense,
trembly feeling,
as I tap his shoulder.
He's waiting for me
and
      oh, my life
         I can't NOT see his thighs.

Benjamin turns and gives me
a grin with dimples
—a thing of beauty,
a gift from the gods—
and I find my mind

s

l

i

p

s

to the word
*bite.*

God, I want to
bite his thighs.

"Hop on," he says
with a nod to his back.

I want to ride him
all the way home
but I'm not sure
if it's rude,
considering what I'm thinking
is not what he's offering.

"No, really it's fine," I say.

"OK," says Benjamin,
with a shrug,

which makes
the blood rush
to my cheeks

and down below
I feel a tingle.

"Can I still walk you
home?" he says.

I nod,
my heart in my mouth,
my mind in my underpants.

As we leave,
I see Harriet waiting
outside the principal's office.
She looks worried,
and I feel guilty,
which is annoying
because her drama
has nothing to do with me.

Or not anymore
anyway.
She made it that way.

# The Space Between Us

On the way home,
the space between
Benjamin and me
seems to shrink
as we chat,
until gradually
our shoulders are bumping.

"Have you seen that photo?"
he asks me,
and I think for a moment
he means the naked one of me,
then I wonder if he means
the picture from Harriet
to Mr. B. But then adds,
"Of the black hole?"

And I'm so relieved.
It's cool he's into
the same stuff as me.
Talking to him is so easy.

I nod.
"It blows my mind.
Do you ever think
how we're so lucky?
Like, witnessing
so many things that

the human eye
has never seen.
We're living through history."

"I've never thought about it
like that," he says.
"You're right.
It's so easy
to take for granted
all the amazing things
we've seen
because of photography."

And briefly,
I think about Harriet
and the things people have seen
because of her photography.

# Everything About Him

I like how
when Benjamin talks
his voice goes soft,
like he's singing.

I like how
when he walks
his curly hair bounces,
like he's on the sprung floor of the gymnasium.

I like how
even though they're friends, he knows Jackson
hasn't grown up at all since elementary school.

I like how
he asks what I think about things
that are actually interesting.

I like how
as we walk home
his ideas seem to change
and wrap around mine
so that what we are saying
seems to be creating
some kind of new meaning
in the shrinking space
between us.

I like how
he stops beside
the railings of the park fence again
to kiss me,
just like this morning.

I like
where this is going.

I like everything about him.

# Fingers

As we near my house,
I find
that my mind
wanders from

our conversation,
so I'm not
thinking about
anything much

because all
I want to do
is touch
Benjamin

and it's strangely
peaceful to find
my mind
is mostly
in my fingers.

# How do you get there?

We reach my house,
there's no one home,
and in the doorway,
Benjamin stands
teetering on the threshold
with his dimpled grin
and his chest
rising and falling.

                                    I want to
                                    grab him
                              and pull him in.

Our mouths say "goodbye,"
but our bodies linger
because
(I think)
our fingers
have other ideas.

                        "Do you want to come in?
                          There's nobody home."

"OK." He shrugs
and just like that
he steps in.

He puts down his bag

and takes off his sneakers.
He's not wearing socks
so it's weird for a second
because Benjamin's
**naked feet**
are touching my carpet.

I've seen bare feet
a million times before,
but now they seem
completely obscene.

I stare at his feet
and start to feel hot,
so I take off my shoes
and I take off my socks
and I take off my sweater.
And the top button of my shirt opens,
and Benjamin's eyes
fall on my bra.

                    "Are you thirsty?" I ask.

Benjamin nods
and swallows so loudly
I actually hear it.

I go to the kitchen,
but all I'm thinking is:
How do we get from
here
          to
                              there?

Back in the hall,
I hand him a glass and
as it passes between us
it slips through our fingers,
so Coke
splatters our shirts
and goes on the carpet.

"Shit," says Benjamin.

                              "Shit," I say.


Then we both look down
at our wet shirts
(and if his shorts
were clinging before,
now they are wet-look Lycra).

"This is my only rugby shirt.
I should try to wash it."

                    "Then you should take it off,"
                         I say, giggling a little
                            at the words coming
                              out of my mouth.


"We both should,"
he says, lifting his shirt
over his head.

                         "OK." I laugh.
                    My heart beats so hard

beneath the stained shirt
that I can see my skin trembling
as I undo the buttons.

"Should we go to your room?"
he says, looking around.

I shake my head.
I don't want to move,
to break the moment.
"My parents won't be
home for hours."

Then we look at each other,
still smiling from laughing,
but now we're both blushing.

I think we both know
we're about to go

**there.**

And just like Harriet
said it would be,
as we press
our hot chests,
skin to skin
body to body,
I find that I can
just be me.

Then our lips touch,
and we're kissing

with tongues,
and the breath from our lungs
mingles together.
This is so much more fun
than I thought it would be.

# "I want to bite your thighs"

I murmur.

Oh my god.

Did I *say* that?
*Can* I say that?
Can I even *think* that?

But,
"OK,"
Benjamin says.
Then, "This is fun."

# His Thighs

From a distance,
Benjamin's thighs are statuesque,
the thighs of Michelangelo's *David*,
sculpted perfection.

Yet now I feel them,
they're bulge and flex,
heat and sweat,
as I
  press my cheeks
    against his flesh
  and lick his skin,
which tastes
of him.

I touch my teeth to him,
and
bite
his
thighs.

# Giggling

"Wow," I say, giggling
as my whole body takes in
the hot and the wet of his
bare chest.

"Shit," says Benjamin,
giggling. "Are we allowed
to do this on a school day?"

> "I'm OK with it
> if you're OK," I say,
> giggling.

Benjamin nods,
smiling.
"I'm definitely OK."

> I like this about him.
> Despite the intensity
> of what our hands are doing,
> we're both still giggling.

# Fun

I expected my first time
getting serious like this
to be *so* serious.
But it's *so* not.

In fact Benjamin and I are
still laughing,
gasping at the fun of
using nothing but our hands
and fingers
and our joined solar plexuses
to make each other come.

# Crime Scene

We lie on the floor
of the hall
of my house,
panting
and laughing.

A smashed vase
and broken glass
and our discarded tops
decorate the wet carpet.

"That *was* fun,"
Benjamin says.

                  "It was," I agree,
              sitting up slightly,
                   taking it in.
           "It looks like a crime scene."

Benjamin props himself up too,
and looks at the mess
of flowers and clothes,
laughing,
then,
at the same moment,
we both look down
at Benjamin's hands
and see blood
on his fingers.

"Shit!" he says, getting up,
turning his hands over,
searching for a cut.

My stomach drops.
I touch the tips of my fingers
to my underpants
and from the sticky feeling
know what's happened.

I cringe
and shrink
and desperately try and try to think
of a way to make this
situation go away.

Benjamin looks terrified,
"I don't think I'm bleeding,"
he says.
"Have I hurt you?"

"No," I say,
dying inside.
"I'm OK. It's just . . .
that time."
I scrunch up my face.
Benjamin's silent,
and I glance at him,

and he looks
at me
blankly.

Oh my god.
I'm going to have to
explain this frankly.

"You know,
it's that time of the month . . .
I got my period?
It's menstrual blood."

WHY did my first time
saying *menstrual blood*
outside of health class
have to also be
the first time
anything remotely sexy
has ever happened to me?

"Ohhh!" he says slowly,
looking between his bloody
fingers and me.
"I see."

# It's Only Blood

Benjamin doesn't move,
and he doesn't look at me.
"Are you OK?" he asks.
"Did I . . . hurt you?"

> "No," I say,
> shaking my head.
> "It was . . . good."

"Are you sure?" he says,
still looking down at his fingers.

> I don't know
> whether he's talking
> about hurting me
> or satisfying me.
> This is so embarrassing.
> "I'm really OK," I say.
> "It's just my period."

"Phew," he says, nodding
like he's trying to catch up.
"I guess it's only blood."

> "Yeah . . ." I say.
> "Totally. Only blood."
>
> I know it is only blood,
> but no one else
> usually sees your period.

"Ugh," I say. "I'm dying."

"It's fine," he says,
though it feels like he's
trying to convince himself
as much as me.
"I've got a sister,
remember?"
Then he laughs,
"Which in this context
makes me sound
like a giant weirdo."

I laugh nervously.
"It's OK; I know
what you mean."

"Phew." He grins.
"I just mean . . .
I know about periods and stuff.
I don't mind blood.
It's biology.
I'm actually thinking
about studying medicine
in college."
He finally looks up at me,
grinning widely.

"Weirdo alert,"
I say, grinning back.

Benjamin laughs
and then we're both
giggling, when suddenly

the mail slot clatters
and we both jump up,
scrambling from the floor,
diving for cover,

as nothing more
than a newspaper
lands in the hall.

We look from the paper
to each other.

                    I've managed to grab
            my dad's reflective cycling vest
                        to cover myself,
                    even though I'm only
                        half undressed.

But Benjamin has
a Kim Kardashian selfie book,
with a massive picture of
her face and boobs,
over his crotch,
covering the wet patch
on his underwear.

                        I snort as he

looks down
to see what he's holding.

"Ugh!" he says. "Why do you
have this?!"

I cover my mouth,
laughing at the sight of him.
"Harriet gave it to me
for my birthday.
She thought I'd like it,
because it's about
photography,
but I think she actually
wanted it for herself."

"Now I really need
to wash my hands," he says.

"The bathroom's up there."

He backs up the stairs,
with Kim Kardashian's face
still held in place.
"I didn't know you were
into photography."

"I'm not," I say. "Harriet is.
But we do take photos
of the moon and stars together.
I'm kind of the astronomer
and Harriet's the photographer.
I'll show you if you like."

# Afternoon Stargazing

We sit cross-legged
on my bedroom carpet,
his rugby shirt
under my hair dryer,
me fully dressed,
him wearing only a towel.

"This is a bit unfair,"
Benjamin says,
over the warmth
of the electric whirr.

He waves the hair dryer
at his shirt

                    which I'm holding.
                       It is billowing,
            rippling over my fingers,
         releasing the smell of him.
           I want to kiss him again.

          I show him Harriet's and my pictures
                  of the night sky,
            collected on the account
           she made where we post
           anything good we take.

"They're amazing," he says.
"When do you do it?"

"Whenever it's dark.
Sometimes we have sleepovers,
then get pastries
from the bakery
on Main Street.
It opens at, like, two a.m."

"You get up that early?"

"Hell, no," I say.
"We stay awake that late!"

"Just doing astronomy?"

I laugh. "Actually,
mostly talking."

"What do you talk about?"

"Everything."
It used to be true.

"Everything?"

I nod. "Pretty much."

I wish we weren't
in this stupid fight.
Tonight, when Benjamin's gone,
who am I going to tell
about this first boy thing?

"What about you?
Who do you talk to?

Jackson?"

"No way," he says.
"We've been friends
forever, but I don't tell him
*anything*. I'm close to my sister.
But she's in California now.
She's a programmer."

                    "California must be nice."

"Yeah, for her," he says.
"I really miss her."

Benjamin looks around my room,
then says, "Nice curtains,"
nodding toward the window
and laughing again.

                    I look at my curtains
                            that I've had
                        since I was seven.
                    The illustrated stars,
                    planets, and rockets
                            so familiar
                    I almost don't see them.

                    I read the exclamations
                    scattered all over them,
                    like *TOTALLY COSMIC!*
**BLAST OFF!** and
                    *INTERGALACTIC!*

"Yeah," I say. "I was a bit
obsessed with space."

"And you took
all those photos
you just showed me
because you're not anymore?"

"OK," I say. "I'm still obsessed.
Anyway, I'm allowed to express
myself in my own room."

"I said they're *nice*."
He grins. "In fact, they're
*totally cosmic*."

"Your shirt is ready."

He turns off the hair dryer,

and I quickly sniff
his warm-shirt smell
before handing it back.

"So . . . space?" he asks,
pulling his top over his curly hair.
"How do you *be* into that?
Other than taking pictures?"

"I'll show you."

We lie beneath the skylight,
and I open an app on my phone

151

that lets you stargaze
(or as close as you can to it)
in broad daylight.

I hold my phone,
heavy and cool in my hot hand,
panning across constellations,
then point it to the waxing moon
in its first quarter.
"It'll be gibbous tomorrow," I say.

"How do you know?"

"Well . . ." I hesitate,
wondering how nerdy to be.
"In the northern hemisphere,
a waxing moon is illuminated
on the right.

There's a lunar eclipse next week,
which means there'll be
a blood moon.
It'll be amazing."

"Cool," he says. "Could I see
the moon one night? Like,
through your telescope?"

"Sure. We always go up
on the full moon.
Unless it's cloudy,
or the timing isn't right."

"But you can see the stars
any night, as long as it's clear?"

"Yep," I say.
"Weather permitting.
But they're always there.
They're there now, you know.
We don't think about it
because the sun is so bright,
but we're also
bathing in starlight."

"That is . . . *intergalactic!*"
He grins, but I know
he's not being sarcastic.
He actually means it.

# Eye Gazing

We gaze at the stars
            awhile,
but actually,
            it's more interesting
                        gazing at each other.

I didn't think there was
any singular thing
more interesting than
the whole of the rest
of the universe.

Benjamin leans closer to me,
narrows his eyes, and says,
"I can actually see
the strands of muscle
that make up the front
pigmented fibrovascular layer
of your iris."

                        "Wow," I say, my crush
                        on Benjamin extending.
                        "I didn't think this was possible,
                        but are you an even bigger
                                    nerd than me?"

"No way," he says,
pointing over at the window.
"Exhibit A: curtains."

# Chicken Thighs

Most nights Dad cooks
while I talk about my day
until Mom gets home,
but tonight, I stay in my room,
waiting until I absolutely have to
go to the kitchen.

Just before seven,
Dad calls me:
"Frankie! Dinner is served!"

Mom puts her laptop bag down
and comes over to kiss me
before sitting down opposite me.

"How was school?" she asks,
        from far away,
        across the table,
        and the galaxy.

"Yes!" says Dad.
"Tell us everything."

                        I am silent.
                I can hardly tell them
            "I walked home with a boy"
                                    or
            "I got my period on him"
                                and
            I definitely cannot risk

letting slip
"I bit
that boy
(on his rugby-tight thighs)
(in our hallway)
(naked)
(and spilled Coca-Cola)
(and had an orgasm)
(that's when I got my period)
(on his fingers)."

So I just say,
"Good, thanks."

"Did Mr. B read your application?"
she asks, pushing her glasses up
her nose with one finger.

"I've just sent it," I say.
"He said he'll give me
my reference on Friday."

"Excellent!" Dad smacks
me on the back.
"Harry's applying too,
isn't she?"

I don't want to talk
about Harriet,
so I just nod.

"We are so proud of you,"
Mom says.

"I know," I say,
and try not to think about
what I really did today
as I bite
into Dad's famous
barbecued chicken thighs.

# A Picture

I'm in bed at 10 p.m.
when my phone goes *ting*.
I sweep it up, caressing it.
I know it's him.

**Benjamin**
Thinking bout you

**Me**
Me too

**Benjamin**
Send me a pic?

And those four little words
make my insides
go squish.

Benjamin:
with godlike thighs,
a delicious grin,
and naked feet,
inside his shoes,
and clever thoughts
inside his head,

wants a picture
of me.

# Selfie

I take a few.
I look all right,
but then the questions start
  like:

      How much skin?
      Pajamas in?
      Straps or skin?

        Lying down
        or sitting up
        or not in bed?

          I think
          about Benjamin.

          I licked his skin,
          I bit him,
          I menstruated on him.

          He said, "It's only blood,"
          and laughed at my curtains
          and loved my pictures of the moon.

Then I remember
the picture Harriet
took of me
under the trees
after things started
happening with Benjamin and me
at the ice rink that night.

I find it,
and that's the one
I send him.

Straightaway, it says
**Benjamin is typing . . .**

**Benjamin**
You are so pretty.
Here's one of me.
Just for you.
Night x

He's in bed,
smiling,
with bare shoulders.
I can't get enough of it.
I stare and stare and stare
at it, until my eyes are tired,

and I sigh
and lie back
on my bed,
my phone pressed
against my chest,
the weight of it
pinning me to this
perfect moment.

# PART
# TWO

# The Fundamentals of Physics

Harriet steps out her front door
at the exact same moment as me,
and I imagine on another day
telling her about Benjamin
and what we did,
and the pictures we exchanged
late at night in bed,
but instead she raises
her middle finger at me
and says, "Bitch."

"Takes one to know
one," I say, and turn
the other way.
She's the one
who took a photo of me
in the showers at school.
Talk about bitchy.

I don't need her anyway.
She said I'm nothing to her.
Well, she can be nothing to me.

I walk to school with
the wind in my hair.

The morning sun
glistening on the dew.
I feel #NoFilter fine.
I'm textbook.
I've totally got it.

On his street
Benjamin is waiting for me,
leaning against the brick wall
outside his house.
He stands straight up
and crosses to meet me.

> "Good morning," I say.
> "Nice to see you."

"Hey, you," he says,
smiling, and walking beside me.
"Sleep OK?"

> "I did," I say.
> "You?"

"Well," he says,
our feet in sync.
"I had this
weird dream that you and I
were in space."

> "Like astronauts?" I say,
> glancing at him sideways.

"Actually, we weren't
exactly in space,

we were swimming around
like there was no gravity."

                "With space suits on?"

"Nope."

                "So we were dead."

Benjamin laughs.
"We were
sort of in a drawing . . ."
He hesitates,
"like your curtains . . ."

                I laugh, nudging him.
                  "You dreamed
                about my curtains!"

"Well, they are
*totally cosmic!*"

                *"You dreamed about*
                *my curtains,"* I crow,
                loving the feeling
                of *my things*
                making it into
                *his subconscious.*

"Did you dream
about me?"
Benjamin asks,

                and I wish I could lie,
                but I hardly ever

remember my dreams.
"I thought about you.
A lot," I say.

Then Benjamin leans in,
with this sweet uncertainty,
and very lightly kisses me.

I kiss him back
and feel a rush
of blood to my head
at us kissing
so casually,
so comfortably,
so familiarly.

*Life is amazing.*

Our lips part,
and that's when I get
the *ooze-squish-blob*
of dripping blood:
impending f
l
o
o
d.

(How the frick did my
ultra-plus tampon
fill up so quick?)

Benjamin takes my hand
and we start to walk,

our swinging arms
bumping lightly,
but

I'm walking funny.
I cannot let my underwear
and tights meet,
because once they do,
the blood will find
a path.

Then
I
will
be
done for.
That's fluid dynamics.

(The Period Woman
who came in sixth grade said,
"It's only blood,"
"just a quarter-cupful,"
"nothing to be embarrassed about."
But when did she last try to
flirt with her underwear
filling with blood?)

"You're limping,"
says Benjamin.
"You OK?"

"I pulled my . . . thigh,"
I say with #InstantBlush.
The first word that came to mind.
(Obviously.)

We take one step.
His arm s l i d e s under mine.
"Here, you can lean on me."

My heart goes squish.
Then, with one wrong step,
my underwear and tights meet.

I walk beside Benjamin,
our bodies touching,
knowing I now have
wet and sticky

*thighs.*

"What?" says Benjamin.

"What?" I say.

"You said 'thighs.'"

"I don't think I did."

"You definitely did."

But I don't want to bring up
my period,
after what we did.
So I limp on.

"I can give you a piggyback,"
he says. "It would help
with my training."

But I just shake my head

and say, "No, thanks,"
hoping I can keep my secret
in my underpants.

At the school gate,
Benjamin looks around,
then very quickly
pecks me
on the cheek.
"See you later?"

"Sure," I say,
tingling where the tickly
feeling of his kiss
on my cheek
briefly distracts me
from the creeping,
crampy feeling
in my womb.

Then I hurry away,
calculating how long
it will take
to get to the bathroom
and change my tampon
and get to class.
#Embarrassing

# Rumors

I'm in history class, and Ms. Wyse
isn't there yet, but from the tone
of the pre-class murmur
there's definitely
    *something*
        *happening,*
and I wonder
if Harriet's selfie
sent to a teacher
is still going strong.
It could go the week,
or maybe make the leap
to other schools
and go on and on.

Benjamin's at the back
with the boys.
He avoids my gaze
as I sit beside Marie,
who has stopped ignoring me
since Harriet took that photo
of me in the showers.


Then
    I
        hear
    one
        word

above

       the

white

    noise

of

    gossiping.


P e r i o d .


I whip my head around
to look at Benjamin.


I stare at him.
He must be able to tell
I'm looking at him,
but he will not
look at me.
He hides his face
behind his history book.


I check my phone,
but there's nothing.
Bethany leans in to Leylah
and Marie,
glancing at me,
unsure if she's allowed
to talk to me.


  "Gossip!" she says,
   then cups her hand,
   whispering,
    gradually more quietly.
    "Jackson just told me

Benjamin
    fingered someone
    on their *period*!"

"Ew!" Leylah bursts.
"That's DISGUSTING."

                The still-damp patch in my underwear
                            is pressing coldly
                            against my skin,
                            and I'm sweating.

                            I watch Marie
                as her face bunches up
                            in disgust
                        at the gossip.

                            About me.

                        And I swallow
                        the acid feeling
                creeping up my throat.

Benjamin told *Jackson*
what we did?

I try to imagine Benjamin,
just now,
after he kissed me,
*b r a g g i n g*
to Jackson and the boys
about getting off with me,
about touching me,
about fingering me.

The betrayal freezes me,
physically.
I turn again, jerkily,
to try and make Benjamin
look
at
**me.**

But he won't.

Bethany's saying,
"That's so grim!"

And Marie asks the others,
"What do you think of him?"

"He's cute," says Leylah.

"I wonder if he's available,"
says Bethany.

Then Harriet looks at me slyly,
and says, "He likes you,
doesn't he, Frankie?"

She's too close to the truth.
"I think I preferred it
when you weren't
talking to me."

"Someone's got PMS,"
she says, making
the others snicker.

None of them consider
it could actually have been me.

The one thing I have
at the moment
is that no one
seems
to know
it was me.

Still, I can't stop imagining
all the boys this morning,
laughing as Benjamin
made our intimacy
*something funny*.

The thing is, it was funny.
But it was funny between us.

# Break Time

It's all anyone talks about
in their groups at break,
because everyone revels in
the opportunity to be
disgusted by something.

"It's disgusting!" Leylah says.

"I bet it went
*e v e r y w h e r e !*"
Harriet says,
nibbling an Oreo,
then making a face,
like she's going to faint
(which she actually did
in eighth grade
when we dissected a frog
and she saw blood).

"Can we drop it now?"
Marie asks,
unwrapping a granola bar.
"Some of us are about to eat."

Harriet gives Leylah a look,
which points the finger
at Marie.

"Who would do
something like that?"

Harriet asks,
and I notice
her looking over
at Jackson,
who is probably
discussing the same thing
with his friends.

Harriet looks at me.
"Come on, Frankie,
tell us what you think."

                    I want to say,
                    "It's only blood,"
         but that would be as good
                    as a confession,
                        so I say,
         "I thought you weren't
                    talking to me."

She gives me
a dirty look
and says,
"Why are you standing
near me, then?"

                    "I must have
                        forgotten
                    how much I
                    dislike you,"
                I say, shrugging.
                    Then I leave
         to search the crowd

on the concrete schoolyard
for Benjamin
to ask him
why he blabbed
our secret.

# Popularity

At the end of break,
I spot him
right before we go in
to health.

He stares at me
like a wild animal
caught in the open,
and I want to hurt him.

I go to the corner
of the building,
beckon him with my head
to follow me.

I fight the urge to
**SHOUT AT HIM.**
"You told Jackson?"

"I didn't! I swear."

"Well, you told someone!
Or how does the
whole school know?"

"I thought it was you."

"Me?" I say,
looking at his panicked face.
"Why would *I* tell *anyone*?"

"Not even Harriet?
You said you tell
her everything?"

                              "We're not talking."

"Shit," he says,
flattening his curly hair
beneath his interlaced fingers.
He has a circle of sweat
in each armpit.

                    "Did you tell the boys
                    you were with me?" I ask.

But he just breathes out,
head back,
looking at the sky.

                         "Benjamin!
              What did you tell them?"

"There he is!" Jackson yells,
striding around the corner.
"Up top! You dawg."

                    I want to melt into nothing,
                         become invisible,
                    try to not be standing here
                         in broad daylight,
                              with Benjamin,

who
scowls
at Jackson,

leaving him
        hanging.

        (The first decent thing
        he's done
        all morning.)

"Come on, Benji.
Tell us who you fing—"

                "Get lost, Jackson,"
                Benjamin says,
                glancing briefly
                at me.
        But that makes
        Jackson notice me.

                        There's nowhere to hide.

"Not her?" he says,
looking me over dismissively.
"Harriet told me she's frigid.
Come on, who was it?
Does she go to our school?"

Benjamin stands up
a little straighter.
"I said, get lost, Jackson."
He laughs lightly.
"I'll see you in class,
you ass."

Jackson looks me up
and down

one more time,
then leaves

                              me feeling
                       like I've been
               slapped in the face.

              Harriet told Jackson I'm *frigid*?
                What else did she tell him?
                    Why was she even
                     talking to him?

"See?" Benjamin says to me.
"There's no way
I'd tell *him* anything."

                  But I just stand there,
                    feeling lonely,
                        thinking,
                I can't trust anybody.

"At least no one knows
it was you," he whispers.
"*Everyone* is talking about me."

                     This is true.
                    Everyone *is*
                talking about him.
            But it's not embarrassing.

                     "Yeah," I say,
                realizing something.
            "And you've never been
              more popular."

# The Hunt

Later, in the lunchroom,
I hear Jackson's voice,
loud above
the clatter of cutlery
and chatter of the crowd.

"Come on, girls.
Who is on the rag?"
he howls,
a bloodhound
with a scent.

The girls all scream
with shrill denial.
  "Oh my god!"
    "Not me!"
  "Not me!"
     "Don't be gross."
   "It's disgusting."

But not one of them says,
**It's only blood.**

     **It is only blood.**
      **Only blood.**

      But neither do I.
      I just eat my fries
      at an empty table,

wishing I had a
packed lunch today.

Harriet doesn't
bother me.
She's too busy
asking everyone
who they think
this mystery girl might be,

making sure
the gossip stays on this
juicy new topic
and doesn't come back to her
and her ridiculous selfie.

On my way to the bathroom
before the last class
there's a crowd
gathered outside
the girl's bathroom,
which is so annoying
because I need to
change my tampon.

Clutching a new one
in my pocket,
I try to sidle through,
but in the middle of it all,
I end up next to Benjamin.

"Frankie!" he whispers loudly
in my ear. "You should

get out of he—"
"WRITE YOUR NAME
HERE IF YOU'RE ON THE RAG!"
a voice shouts.
Jackson.

He's sticking a piece of paper
to the bathroom door.
"Come on, ladies," he shouts.
"Own up. Who's riding
the crimson wave?"

He scans the crowd,
then stops on Harriet.
"What about you?" he says.
"Everyone knows you're
dirty, you dick tease."

Harriet scoffs at him.

"I thought I wasn't your type
anyway. We're not family?"

"What's that supposed to mean?"
Jackson throws back.

"Those girls from your threesome?
That photo you showed us
with them kissing your cheeks?
They're your cousins, right?"

A few people titter,
and Jackson looks furious,

and I think he's really
about to go for her,
but then she

turns around
and surveys the crowd
like she's the queen and
judge of everything
and says, "Maybe it was Marie.
She's always had a heavy flow."

I gasp.

I know Harriet is
sometimes mean,
but I cannot believe she
is directing her cruelty at Marie.

(Marie got her period first,
and all us girls know
it's heavy,
but for Harriet
to break Marie's privacy,
to tell *everybody*,
is almost beyond belief.)

Harriet did think
it was funny to send
a sexy selfie to Mr. B
and to take a photo of me
in the shower.

"Harriet!" I say
as I shake my head.

"What?" she says,
pretending she doesn't know
what she's done.
She should just say sorry.

I take a step back
and catch my heel on
Benjamin's bag
and stumble back,
        my hands flailing,
                my tampon skittering,
                        rolling and stopping
                            at the
            bathroom door.
I land on the floor.

Harriet gasps, then
        sees my face,
        sees Benjamin,
both of us blushing.

She raises an eyebrow,
then looks at
him,
        eyes narrowing.

"Frankie," she says,
her face changing.

The crowd falls silent.

                        "Leave it, Harry."

"It wasn't her,"

she says to Jackson quickly.
"She's practically a *nun*,"
she tells everyone, laughing.
"Do nuns even have periods?"

              "Why are you helping him?"
                I say, nodding to Jackson.

"Bitch fight!" Jackson cries,
but no one joins him;
everyone is looking
from me to
Harriet.

Then Marie goes up
to the bathroom door
and picks up the tampon
from the floor,
then with one swift tug,
tears the paper down from the door.

"Hey!" says Jackson.
"Who said you could do that?"

"Statistically," says Marie,
facing Jackson.
"About a quarter of
menstruating women
are having their period at any one time,
so this"—she waves the paper—
       "is bullshit.

      And anyway,
      do you know how boring it is,

what you're doing?
Periods are normal.
You're the weird thing."

Then she scrunches the paper up
and throws it
at the trash can next to me.
"Everyone ignore him."

"It was Marie!"
Jackson hollers.
"Benjamin fingered
slutty little Marie
when she was
on the rag!"

I feel guilty,
and relieved
she's taken
the heat off me,
because my cheeks
are threatening
to give me away.

Marie looks angry,
but Jackson is still going.
"I can smell your pussy
from here, Marie.
Blood and"—
he sniffs the air—
"cum."

There are a few laughs,
and briefly,

I see Marie's mask falter.
Not anger . . .
perhaps humiliation?
Or regret for sticking
out her neck.

No one is saying anything.
Not even Harriet.
She's just letting Marie take it.

                                    I pick myself up
                                        and say,
                                "As if you'd know what
                                a vagina smells like."

Jackson swings around
to look at me.
"The nun! She speaks!"

                        "The closest you've ever been
                    to the inside of a girl's underpants
                            is right where you are now.
                    Lurking outside the girls' bathroom."

Then **everyone** laughs
                                at him,
                                    because of me.

"I've just remembered,"
Jackson says,
regaining the crowd,
"I did see Benjamin
with someone earlier.
What were you two

whispering about,
*Freaky Frankie?*"

"We weren't whispering,"
Benjamin says quickly.

Far. Too. Quickly.

The color of my cheeks
is all Jackson needs.
I swallow
loudly.

"It *WAS* Frankie!"
Jackson screams.
"You.

Dirty.

Sluuuuuuuut!"

For a moment
I stand still.
I can survive this.
If I don't move,
Jackson will back down.
But then

everyone turns around
to look at me,
and in the crowd I see
Leylah and Bethany,
and on their faces
I see a flicker of
something.

Disgust?

Do they think
I'm disgusting?

I am breaking.
I don't even stop
to pick up my backpack.

I run,
crying,
crumbling.
I am disgusting.

# Harriet's Advice

In the other girls' bathroom,
I pull my feet up,
crouching on the lidless seat,
my f i n g e r s clinging
to the **crusty** rim.
There's no point worrying
about what I'm touching.
*I* am the dirty thing.

"Frankie!" a voice snaps at me
impatiently as the door bangs closed
and angry footsteps approach.

Harriet's hair drapes on the floor
as her face peeps
under the stall door.

She stands and sighs.
"Mr. Guerra made me
come get you.
He knows you're in here.
If you don't come now,
he's going to mark you
down as cutting."

                              "I don't care," I say,
                                 trying not to sniff.

"You can't hide in here all day,"
Harriet says. "Don't make

it *worse* than it needs to be."

"Harriet,
you have no idea
what you're talking about,
so just get lost."

"Come on, Frankie.
Don't be so weak.
You'll get through this.
*I* did."

"It's not the same."

"It's not *that* different."

"It is! What's happening
to me is worse."

"Worse than getting moved
into the slow class?
Worse than a teacher
telling on you because
he thought you were
trying to flirt with him?"

(Which she was.)

"And everyone seeing
the picture of you?"

I can't believe she thinks
she's the victim.
*She* sent it.

"Toughen up.
Just tell everyone
to grow up."

                              "I just got called a slut.
                                       For nothing."

"Well . . ." she says, pausing.
She's loving this.
"Not *nothing*.
You did let Benjamin
*finger you*
on your period.
You're not even going
out with him!"

                              "What the hell, Harriet?
                                Since when were you
                      the judge of what's decent?"

"I'm just saying.
It wasn't *nothing*."

                              "You *sexted* a teacher,"
                      I shout through the door.
                          "That's so much worse."

"But much less slutty."

                                    "You told Jackson
                                  that I'm *FRIGID*."

"Well you proved me wrong,
didn't you."

"Just leave me alone."

"I'd love to.
I'll let Mr. Guerra know
you'll be crying in here
all afternoon over nothing."

"If you only came here
to tell me my problems
are nothing, you've done that."

"I came here to tell you
you're making a mistake
hiding away
like you've done something
to be ashamed of.
Come back to class
and this will blow over.

Oh, and by the way,
you left your backpack in the hall.
I put it in your locker.
It was decorated
with sanitary pads.
I peeled them off.
*You're welcome*."

"Are you done?"

"No," she says.
"One more thing.
Stop being such a baby."

# Baby

At home that night
I open all my chats,
and I mute Harriet
on every one of them,
then set my phone
to silent anyway.
I don't want to hear
from anyone again
until morning.

I curl into Mom
while she reads
a lab report
on the sofa,
and I weep,
cradled in the crook
of her body,
like the baby
Harriet says I am.

Mom holds me close,
waits as I sob,
then dry my eyes
enough to speak.

Then finally
I tell her everything
Harriet did, like about her

sexting Mr. B,
texting me during class,

taking a photo of me in the shower
and pretending to send it to Mr. B.

I tell her everything
Harriet did, but I leave
out all the
stuff about me
and Benjamin.
(Obviously.)

There's plenty
for Mom to be
really shocked about,
which makes me feel better.

"That all sounds pretty serious,"
Mom says. "I guess that's
why Lola grounded her."

"How do you know that?"

"I heard Lola shouting at her.
I hope they're both OK.
Has something happened
to make Harriet act this way?"

"No," I say, annoyed with
her for being so reasonable.
So understanding.
So kind to Harriet.
The bitch.

"Everything is caused
by *something*," says Mom.

I wish she wasn't always
so rational.
"Can I stay at home
tomorrow?" I ask.

"No," Mom says. "You're not sick.
Besides, you're seeing Mr. B.
To talk about your application."

I was so excited
about that before.
But not anymore.
Now I'm just going
through the motions.
"Can I bring lunch tomorrow?"

"Of course," she says.
"That will give you a chance to talk to
Mr. B, to see what he's
put in his reference!"

"I still don't want to go in."

"Just talk to her about it,"
she says, like I knew
she would eventually.
"Or do you want me to
knock and talk to Lola?"

"No!" I say, because

Harriet might have told
her mom *everything*.

"Don't talk to her at all.

Even if you see her.
Otherwise I'll never tell you
anything ever again."

"OK," she says,
drawing a cross on her heart.
"Do you want me to
read your application?"

"No," I say. "It's OK.
It's basically ready.
I just need Mr. B's
reference tomorrow."

"That's my girl."

I smile,
but I'm not really sure
what kind of girl
she thinks I am.
Or what kind of girl
I actually am.

I pick up my phone,
instinctively thinking
about discussing it
with Harriet
before remembering
we're not talking.

Then our fight
repeats on me,
weighs down on me,
horribly.

And instead I go to bed
feeling heavy
and wondering whether
Harriet and I
can ever
get back
to being
best friends again.

After all,
to her,
I'm nothing.

# Seeing Red

My phone is vibrating:
My morning alarm?

Muscle memory
makes me reach
out my fingers.
I try to snooze it,
but it won't stop.

There's a *ting*
and a *chirp*
and a *ding*.

Notifications
come firing in.
I open my eyes
and blink at the screen.

And all I see is
**red.**

Almost every **app**
has **a** little red dot
like **a** gunshot wound.

WTF?

# Meme

Someone
has made
a meme
of me.

## I GOT FINGERED ON MY PERIOD

The picture of me
I sent to Benjamin.
(The one that Harriet
took under the
ice rink parking lot trees.)

A
picture
of two
bloodied
fingers.

## AND I BLOODY LOVED IT

# Choices

7:31 a.m.
"Frankie! I'm making oatmeal."

My favorite.
Mom's only in the kitchen,
but she's light-years away.
I hug my knees
and try
and try
and try
not to cry.

7:35 a.m.
"Have a good day, Frank!"
Dad shouts.

He slams the door,
leaving,
not knowing
I'm breaking.
I can't go to school today.

7:39 a.m.
"Frankie! It's ready!
Shall I bring some to you?"

"No!" I shout.
Like a flash, I'm moving.
"I'm coming down."

I get dressed,
use cover-up
around my splotchy,
blotchy,
puffy
eyes.

I pick up some tampons
then go downstairs.
There's no point crying.
No point saying I'm too sick to go in.
I pick up my backpack.

"I have to go in early
to see Mr. B," I lie.
It's surprisingly easy.

"You still need to eat,"
she says, putting down
her spoon.

"I'll eat this on my way,"
I say, grabbing a banana,
trying not to face her.

"What about your teeth?"
she says.

"Brushed them already."

"Don't forget your lunch!"
She points to a box,
on the counter.

She's made me
lunch,
just like she used to
for elementary school.
"Thanks, Mom," I say.

She's cut my sandwiches
four ways.
It makes
my heart ache.

"I'm proud of you,"
she calls after me.

If only she knew.

# How Bad Can It Be?

Outside, I let myself feel it.
My feet pound the sidewalk,
rage and injustice
boiling up from a place
I didn't even know existed.

I only sent that picture
to Benjamin.
So I know
        this was him.
No one has had my phone.

I swipe past the hundreds
of notifications to call
        Benjamin.

It r i n g s
and  r i n g s
and           he           doesn't      a n s w e r.

He said he didn't mind.
He said it's *biology*.
He said, "It's only blood."

How dare he ignore me?

I pass the railings of the park
where only yesterday morning,
Benjamin stopped
        and kissed me.

I look down at my phone
and see the pictures again,
placed beside one another,
making me seem
so disgusting,
and another wave of self-loathing
washes over me.

I sit down in an alleyway
and read everything,
my blood boiling,
until I've seen it all
and it's part of me.

I'm disgusting.

I'll just go get my reference
and then leave.
How bad can it be?

# How Bad It Can Be

I go through the gates.
  The static crackle of
  goSSip
  flows ahead of me.

The crowd parts slightly,
laughter and hollers
following me.

Marie shoulders her way
out from a group
to walk with me.

"You're here!" she says.

      "Yeah," I say.

"I can't believe it."
She links my arm.
"I didn't think you'd come."

    "What did you think I'd do?"
    I ask, genuinely interested,
    because I have no idea
    how to handle this.

"Stay at home.
That's what I'd do.
You're so brave."

"Where's Harriet?" I say.

"She's over there."
Marie nods behind her.
"Don't talk to her,
it'll only make it worse."

I wonder for a second
what she means,
but then I see Harriet

talking to Leylah,
and she sees me
and

even though she must know
what's happened to me
she turns her back on me
and walks off without Leylah.

My heart sinks.
Is Harriet still
not talking to me?

"Ignore her," says Marie.

But I'm barely listening
because all I'm thinking
is how I need
Harriet now,
but I don't think
I'd be able to get
the words out.

Marie leads me
through the crowd,
staring everyone down.

"Why are you
being nice to me?" I say.

"Because you don't
deserve this," she says.

"Thanks, Marie.
Have you seen Benjamin?"

She shakes her head.
"What a blabbermouth.
If he is here,
he's going to get
a load of shit from us.
He did leak it, didn't he?"

"Well, *I* didn't tell
anybody," I say numbly.

"That's what we thought,"
she says, nodding.
"And Harry,
she's getting shit from me
today."

"Thanks," I say.
It's nice at least Marie can see
that right now
what I need
is my best friend.

Then the bell rings
for homeroom and I stand there,
searching for Benjamin,

but I don't see him.

# Under Siege

After a hellish homeroom,
I slip into an empty classroom
and, leaning against a seventh-grade display
of medieval battle strategy,
check my phone
for the hundredth time.

It's only been a few
seconds since I last looked,
but there is more.

There
     is
          so
               much
                  more.

There's a <u>link</u> in
my DMs
from someone I don't know.
I click it, my skin prickling.
A page loads on
a site I don't know
with a sidebar of threads
slut-shaming celebs.

My page of shames name:
*Freaky Frankie Finger Fun*

**Randy^^Tts**
<u>this dirty little schoolgirl</u> has no shame
let's teach her a lesson

**B0rg3n**
wanna finger fck this <u>slut</u> & sm. SGILF

**Mazzter**
creamin myself over this lil bitch

I cannot breathe.
I cannot see.
    I have no idea
        what
           to
               do.
But then,
footsteps
coming
toward
this room.

Classes will be starting soon,
and here I am in the history room,
under siege.

There's a door behind me.
A closet.
I duck in
and close it
just as I hear
a class

file in,
so
I'm in
the dark
with
old textbooks,
squatting,
quietly,
balancing,
silently,
carefully,
desperately,
hoping not
to be
discovered
here in this
dark
little closet
hiding
from my own
shame
for
an hour
or more.

Then,
finally,
the chairs scrape,
the door bangs,
the noise in the room
diminishes
to silence,

and I open
the closet a crack
to check that the coast is clear.

I have physics right
after morning break.

I listen
as the volume
rises then falls
in the corridors,
and at
the very
last moment
I make a dash for it.

I need my reference,
then I'm going home.

# Nuclear Decay

In physics, there's no space
next to Marie, so I sit at the front.
Maybe Mr. B can protect me.

There are whispers and giggles of
"slut" and "period" until finally
Mr. B comes in and tells Jackson to
sit down and stop clowning around.

We're doing nuclear decay today,
but I'm not staying.

    I've got my own toxic waste.
    This meme has poisoned me,
    invisibly.
    It will never go away,
    just slowly fade,
    halving exponentially.

I just need the right moment
to ask for the reference,
before saying I have to leave.

"Jackson, do the handouts,
please," says Mr. B.

Jackson gets up and smirks at me
as he passes me and trips over me.
"Watch it, dirty," he says,
slapping my back.

I hear a rustle
as something sticky
is attached to me.
I reach my hand around,
and peel it off.
Then bring it back
to look at it
under the desk.

A sanitary pad.

It's so stupid
I should laugh,
but I can feel tears
start to well in my eyes.

I stand up quickly,
hitting my thighs on the desk.
"Sir, I feel faint. Can I leave?"

"Oh," says Mr. B. "Do you want
someone to take you to
the office?" he asks.

"I'll be fine," I say,
swinging my backpack
onto my back,
already at the door,
but

he calls,
"Don't forget this,"

so I have to come
back into the room
with everyone snickering

to take the reference
from his hand.

"I read your application.
It's amazing. Feel better.
I'll send this by email too."

                        Somewhere inside
                I register what he's saying,
but then Jackson shouts,
"Heavy blood loss
can make you feel faint."

                              And I feel
                        disgusting again.


And it is the smallest comfort
that I hear Mr. B saying,
"Jackson, it is not
acceptable to be heckling
fellow students.
Take a seat
and see me
after class."

# Pointless Advice

I google "What to do if you go viral,"
but the answers sound like
it would be a *good thing*.

In health Mrs. Lovelie said,
    "If you're getting bullied online,
    remember C.R.I.
    Confront. Record. Inform."

Who am I supposed to *confront*?
I don't know the people
piling in on me.

Why would I *record* it?
It's already everywhere.

And *inform* who?
Mrs. Lovelie?

I imagine sitting down
in her little room
and explaining how

                                after school
                    (with my nightclub thighs)
                            Benjamin Jones
                                fingered me
                            on my period,
                    then told everyone.
                    And made a meme,
                    which has gone viral,

                                        so I'm getting filthy
                                messages from strangers.

She probably doesn't even
know what a meme is.

There is still Benjamin.
I could confront him.
He's the only one I sent
the picture to, after all.
He either made the meme,
or he gave someone else
that picture of me.

# Doorstep

Benjamin's house
has a red front door.
I approach it slowly,
watching for signs
of life through the windows,
but everything's still.

I walk up the path
and knock
and wait
on the concrete step,
hoping his mom or dad
won't answer, because
all my anger is lined right up,
ready to fire.

I watch a silhouette
approach through
the foggy glass
and feel his imminent
proximity in my guts.
I take a step back,
as though I've been punched.

Benjamin opens
the door a crack
and looks at me
like he can't believe
I'm here.

"Frankie," he says,
looking behind me,
checking the empty street.
"What are you doing here?"

"Well, I couldn't talk to
you in school, could I?
You coward."

"Ah, man," he says,
his hands on his face.
"You went? I'm sorry.
I just couldn't handle it . . ."

"You couldn't handle *it*,
or *me*?"

"No," he says. "It's not like that.
I'm not ignoring you.
I wanted to talk."

"Well, here I am.
What did you want to say?
Sorry for bragging to all your friends?
Or for sending my picture
around to all the boys?
Or was it actually you?"

"Please," he says,
checking the street again.
"Come inside
and we can speak."

I want to talk to him,
but not in his house.
Not on his terms.

"I've been calling you
all morning."

"I don't have my phone,"
he says. "My parents took it.
And they won't be giving it back
anytime soon.
They're ridiculously strict
about school."

"What? Why?
Do they know?"

"No," he says, quickly.
"I tried to skip this morning.
But they caught me.
Made me go to school."

"Then, where were you?"

"I hid in the library,
then came straight home
when they went out.
I've seen how this shit goes down.
There was no way I was going
to school after that meme."

"I did."

"How was it?"

"It was horrible.
Thanks to you.
I can't believe you
blabbed our secret.
It was private."

"I didn't tell anyone!"

"You must have told someone!"

"I promise,
I didn't tell
a soul in school.
I don't know how
this got out."

"Stop lying!
You were the only one
who knew about what we did."

He says his parents
have his phone,
but maybe he just
doesn't want me
to look on it.

Maybe it's in his pocket
with evidence on it.

He probably sent it
to the boys' group message.
Bragged about fingering me.

"Frankie," he says,
reaching out,
trying to touch me.
"Please come in.
Let's not talk
about this out here.
You have to believe me.
I haven't told anyone
in school
anything."

"Then how does Jackson
seem to know everything?"

"I don't know!"

I *don't* believe him.
"Then how did they know
about my period starting?
*I* didn't tell anyone."

"What? Not even Harriet?"

"I told you. We're not talking."

"But . . .
Harriet made the meme."

# Drifting

"Harriet made the meme."

I'm punched in the stomach,
knocked from my orbit.
Set adrift
spiraling
aimlessly,
helplessly.
I cannot speak.
I cannot breathe.
I cannot see.

"Didn't you know?"
Benjamin says,
taking a step closer to me.
Reaching out to touch me.

I step back,
stagger,
stumble,
mumble,
"No, I didn't know."

"She was the first
to post it."
Benjamin looks worried.
"Frankie," he says.
"Do you want to come in?
You don't look well."

I swallow and blink
and think of how
to get away.
I need to see this
for myself.
"I'm fine," I say, turning around.
"I'm going home.
I'll see you soon."

"I'm sorry," he says.
"I thought you knew.
It wasn't me."

My feet are walking,
my brain is whirring,
and my hands are fumbling
in my backpack
for my phone.

Benjamin calls after me,
"I can help.
I'm going to help.
I'll fix it."

But I'm not listening.
His voice fades
as I drift away,
sniffing and scrolling,
head down,
tears falling,
to see for myself.

# Crumbling

I turn the corner
then stop and wipe
my tear-spattered screen
on the sleeve of my shirt
and click on Harriet's page.

And there it is.
Posted last night,
when Harriet
was at home
on her own.
I muted her,
so I didn't see
that it was Harriet
who did this to me.

*This* is why Marie
said she'd give Harriet
shit for me.

I let out a sob
as my knees buckle
and I slide to the ground
and my insides crumble.

# Harriet Did It?

Harriet did it?

Harriet who
on the first day of nursery school,
wet herself
out of pure solidarity because I did?

Harriet who
saved up her allowance
to buy me my favorite
My Little Pony?

Harriet who
hid behind the trees
when I had my first kiss
(with Elliot Miller)
in case I needed her
to rescue me?

Harriet who has lived next door
my whole life,
who knows everything about me
and knows how much this would hurt me?

Did she do it just
to deflect attention
from her selfie sent
to Mr. B?

Harriet was
*that* angry
with me?

I can't *quite* believe it.

# Harriet Did It

I get up and walk home,
my heart hurting,
my temples pounding.
Harriet did say,
"You're nothing to me,"
but I still can't believe
that all those years,
all those secrets
and moments shared,
really don't mean anything to her.

I reach our street and
glance at Harriet's house
right next door
and think about all the times
we've fought before.

Once at the school fair
we agreed to get our
faces painted like bumblebees.
I went first, then she backed out
and claimed she'd never
said she'd do it.
We had a huge fight.

And once she cut the tail
off one of her own My Little Ponys,
then told her mom it was me.
All I did was tell her not to
cut it in the first place.

She did break
Marie's privacy,
telling everyone
about her period
being heavy.

And she took
that shower-picture
of me.

I guess she is this mean.

# Low

I open my phone
and send her a message.

**Me**
This is a new low,
even for you.

And I watch it
        and watch it,
waiting to see
when it's been delivered,
when it's marked read.

But it doesn't change.
Maybe she's muted me.
Or blocked me completely.
Deleted me?
I don't know if I'd even
be able to see if she had
deleted me.

Maybe
to her
I really am nothing.

# Gone

In my room,
I scroll and scroll,
checking to see
the time stamps on all the posts.

But I can't find any
before the one I saw
on her page.
I go back to look at it,
but then
      I can't find it.
         It's gone.
            I check again.
     I search and search.
~~She's deleted it.~~

I don't know what to think.
Maybe she regretted it?
But that doesn't make
me feel any better.
It's too little too late.
It's **everywhere** already.

I hide my phone
under my pillow
where it can't hurt me,
but I can still feel
the lump of it,
pressing into me,

begging me to
look at it.

I move away,
lie on the floor
and try not to think
about how much
Harriet
has
hurt
me,
but it's the only thing
I can think about.

She might have deleted it,
but it's not gone.
I still can't believe
she actually did it.

I
simply
can't
believe
it.

# A Change of Scene

Mom and Dad arrive home together
and ask me why I haven't been
answering my phone.
(Which is ironic,
as they're always telling me
to get off it.)

I briefly wonder
if they've seen
the meme,
but if they had,
I'd know by now.

They ask
if I want to go for pizza,
a Friday-night treat.

I wonder if we'll see
anyone from school.
But I say yes anyway,
because I really need
a change of scene.

# Pizza

The smell of baked dough
envelops me,
as the waitress leads us
to a table
near the open kitchen,
pizza oven full of orange flames.

The waitress gives us menus,
and as she takes our drink order
she looks at me,
her head cocked to the side,
like she's trying
to place me.

                    And I find I'm sweating.
                              OMG.
              Let her not be trying to place me.
                   Let her not recognize me.

Mom and Dad talk about
climate,
plastic,
politics,
and I try to join in,
but I can feel my phone,
in my pocket,
*buzz buzz buzz*ing.

The rule is
no phones when we're eating

but I take it out
and try to read it on my lap.

Dad is onto me.
"So what's new with you?"

"Nothing," I say,
but my insides writhe.
Maybe I'm just hungry.

"And how's Harry?"

Her name stings.
"Call her Harriet.
She's not *your* friend."

"She is!"
He laughs,

but Mom has the decency
at least
to roll her eyes in empathy.

"Did anything happen with
that boy she was texting?"
he asks, eyebrows waggling.

"Dunno," I say.

"Have you two
still not made up?"
Mom asks.

"No," I say.

"You really should talk,"
Mom says.

Then the waitress is back, saying,
"Are you ready to order?"
and looking at me,
her head cocked again,
like she's about to ask
whether she knows me.

                    I order quickly
          and hand her my menu:
                her signal to leave.
          Then look at my phone
                  on my lap again
                   until she goes.

"No phones at the table, remember.
Who are you texting anyway?"
Dad asks, leaning over.

                  "No one," I say,
               putting it away.

"Have you got
a boyfriend?"
he says.

Mom elbows him.
"She'll tell us
if she wants to."

"If she'd be friends with

me on Facebook,
I wouldn't have to ask."

                "No one puts anything
                on Facebook anymore."

"Doesn't stop you looking at it
five hundred times a day," says Dad.
"Anyway, I post things on there."

                "Exactly," I say.

"Harry's friends
with her mom."

                "Just because they're *friends*
                doesn't mean she lets
                her see anything.
                And it's Harriet."

"Oh, come on," says Dad to me.
"You're always on your phone.
And you're not talking to Harry—
Harriet, I just thought you might
have a BF."

                "Ugh!" I say. "Daaaad.
                You don't *say* 'BF.'"

"Why not? I'm just asking.
It would be sweet
if you did."

                Sweet?

The truth
would
crush him.
"I don't have a boyfriend."

"Promise me you'd tell me
if you did?"

"Sure, Dad," I say.

He smiles
and looks so happy

I actually feel OK
for the first time today.

The waitress lowers
a veggie feast in front of me,
then looks at me
and her face changes.

She's placed me.

"Hey! Aren't you—"

"Thank you," I say,
taking the pizza quickly,
panic washing over me.

"—that girl—"

I cough,
nodding frantically
at my parents.

"—from . . ." She glances
at my mom and dad
        and trails off,
                finally understanding.

"Sorry,
thought you
were someone else!"
she says, doing a good
impression of breezy.
"Enjoy your food."

# That Girl

My hands are slippery
on my silverware.
I cut up my pizza
and force it down quickly.
My stomach feels crampy.
I glance around nervously.
I just want to be
back at home,
in my room,
hiding from reality.

Mom and Dad
eat painfully slowly,
then order dessert,
*and* then coffee,
and the evening
stretches ahead of me
like an infinity.

I go to the bathroom
to check my phone,
     and there's the waitress,
     drying her hands.

"I'm so sorry," she says,
touching my arm.
"You're that girl from
the period meme,
aren't you?"

I nod.

"I go to Thomas Jefferson,
in town.
We've all seen it.
Someone said
you're from around here.
You poor thing."

The kitchen bell pings.
"Better go," she says,
her hand on the door.

"By the way,
I think it's really unfair . . .
        what's happening to you."
She smiles kindly.

"You should say something.
Don't let the trolls win."

She pulls the door open,
the smell of pizza
mingling with the chemical
peach of toilet cleaner.

Back at the table,
and later,
in my room,
her words linger.

Not, "what's happened to you,"
        but, "what's *happening* to you."

# The Weight of Words

I wake in the middle of the night
with a horrible dream
clinging damply to my skin.

>   *I was watching my friends,*
>   *Harriet,*
>   *Marie,*
>   *Leylah,*
>   *Bethany,*
>   *watching a screen.*
>   *On it was me.*

>   *They were all cheering*
>   *as horrible things*
>   *were happening to me.*

>   *And I was just watching,*
>   *doing nothing.*

I go to the window,
fueled by the freedom
of being awake
in the dead of night.

I open it, lean out,
and let the breeze
blow away

the clammy weight
of my bad dream.

At the end of the yard,
up in the leaves
of the sycamore tree,
a light is glowing.

What is Harriet
doing up there
at this time of night?
Maybe she can't sleep
because she's actually
feeling guilty?
                She should be.

I can't believe
all the things she's done
recently.

Like sending that selfie
to Mr. B.

And taking that picture
of me in the shower
after PE.

And laughing about
Marie's heavy periods
in front of everybody.

And posting that

horrible meme.
She doesn't think about
the consequences.
She doesn't take responsibility.

Even if she regretted it
and deleted it.
She still did it.

I check my phone
and I can't believe it,
but there's a message
from Harriet.

**Harriet**
It wasn't me.

I glance up at the tree
and feel in my fists
all the things Harriet
has done to me recently.

*This* pathetic text is all
she can say to me?

It's so typical of her.
Avoiding taking
**any** responsibility.

Fury flies from my thumbs
in a frenzy.

**Me**

Is that really the best
you can do?

**Me**

You're pathetic.
I know it was you.

**Me**

I saw it on your page.
Even if you deleted it.

**Me**

You're such
a fucking liar.

**Me**

You're nothing to me.

God it feels good
to get it off my chest.
To say what I think.
To hurt her
like she's hurt me.

I watch as it says

**Harriet is typing . . .**

But then she stops.

And I'm stuck, waiting,
staring out the window

at the green glow
of the lit-up tree house,
amazed my anger
doesn't make
the glass explode.

# Say Something

I wait for ages,
but Harriet doesn't reply.
I go to my bed
and lie down, but I
can't sleep.

I wander mindlessly
onto the page
*Freaky Frankie*
and read more comments
from people about me.

Some are
supporting me,
but they're all
getting trolled
for being nice to me.
Like that waitress said,
I could say something.

I'm so angry
I start typing.

Oh just fuck off and leave me alone. You are all
saying I'm disgusting. I'm a slut. I'm a whore. I got
my period. Girls get periods. It's only blood.
Deal with it. #ItsOnlyBlood

I hit send and switch off
my phone

and
lie back,
try to slow my
breathing.

I try not to think
about the meme.

Instead I try
picturing myself
at the planetarium,
handing in
my application
to Vidhi.

I try
to imagine
her face when
she reads
my essay
about black-hole
photography.

Or what she'd say
if I got the spot.
How it would be,
working there
all summer
alongside her.

But the idea
of Vidhi,
the planetarium,
in fact anything

that isn't the meme

is

                    beyond me.

# Turn Me On

I wake up early.
I reach for my phone,
feeling hopeful,
maybe my comment
has changed the way
everyone is
talking about me.

I want to wait,
to savor the possibility,
but it's calling me,

Turn
Me
On.

It's beckoning my fingers
to pick it up,
and so I do.

I stroke the screen.
I tap red dots.
It suCks me in.
And all I see are images of me
me
me
me me me me me me me me me me me me me

me me me me me me me me me me me me me me
me me me me me me me me me me me me me me
me me me me me me me me me me me me me me
me me me me me me me me me me me me me me
me me me me me me me me me me me me me me
me me me me me me mc mc me me me me me me me
me me me me me me me me me me me me me me
me me me me me me me me me me me me me me
me me me me me me me me me me me me me me
me me me me me me me me me me me me me me
me me me me me me me me me me me me me me
me me me me me me me me me me me me me me
me me me me me me me me me me me me me me
me me me me me me me me me me me me me me
me me me me me me me me me me me me me me
me me me me me me me me me me me me me me
me me me me me me me me me me me me me me
me me me me me me me me me me me me me me
me me me me me me me me me me me me me me
me me me me me me me me me me me me me me
me me me me me me me me me me me me me me
me me me me me me me me me me me me me me
me me me me me me me me me me me me me me
me me me me me me me me me me me me me me
me me me me me me me me me me me me me me
me me me me me me me me me me me me me me
me me me me me me me me me me me me me me
me me me me me me me me me me me me me me
me me me me me me me me me me me me me me
me me me me me me me me me me me me me me
me me me me me me me me me me me me me me
me me me me me me me me me me me me me me

me me me me me me me me me me me me me me
me me me me me me me me me me me me me me
me me me me me me me me me me me me me me
me me me me me me me me me me me me me me
me me me me me me me me me me me me me me
me me me me me me me me me me me me me me
me me me me me me me me me me me me me me
me me me me me me me me me me me me me me
me me me me me me me me me me me me me me
me me me me me me me me me me me me me me
me me me me me me me me me me me me me me
me me me me me me me me me me me me me me
me me me me me me me me me me me me me me
me me me me me me me me me me me me me me
me me me me me me me me me me me me me me
me me me me me me me me me me me me me me
me me me me me me me me me me me me me me
me me me me me me me me me me me me me me
me me me me me me me me me me me me me me
me me me me me me me me me me me me me me
me me me me me me me me me me me me me me
me me me me me me me me me me me me me me
me me me me me me me me me me me me me me
me me me me me me me me me me me me me me
me me me me me me me me me me me me me me
me me me me me me me me me me me me me me
me me me me me me me me me me me me me me
me me me me me me me me me me me me me me
me me me me me me me me me me me me me me
me me me me me me me me me me me me me me
me me me me me me me me me me me me me me
me me me me me me me me me me me me me me
me me me me me me me me me me me me me me
me me me me me me me me me me me me me me

over and over,

only now
my own
words,
my attempt at a defense,
plaster the meme.

"I'm disgusting."
"I'm a slut."
"I'm a whore."

Why did I
write it
like that?

There's a page called
TOP 13 PERIOD GIRL MEMES
and on every one,
my picture has been changed
in some horrible new way.

And in all of them
are the two pictures
next to each other
as though they
belong together.

The picture Harriet took of me
and
those bloodied fingers.

I don't even know
whose hand that is.

Strangers' fingers
supposedly fingered me.
It's so disgusting.
So creepy.

My shaming is still accelerating,
like the universe,
getting bigger,
*faster,*
drawing its energy
from dirty
little
me.

# Friends

I check my messages,
hoping there'll be
something from Benjamin.
There's nothing.

I can't message him
after yesterday.
He should message me.
Say he's sorry.
It's still his fault
that people knew
what happened between
us that afternoon.

He can't even admit it.
He's no better than Harriet.

I think of Harriet's and my fight
in the bathroom at school.
How she suggested
simply denying
that it was her who sent
the email to Mr. B.

This is classic Harriet.
*It wasn't me.*

Deny it.
Avoid it.
Don't take responsibility.

I do have messages
from all the girls
who message me separately,
avoiding PEANUT BUTTER AND JELLY
where it would (obviously)
be awkward.

They're asking if I'm OK.
Telling me that Harriet denies
it was her who posted it.
That they don't believe her.
But it's all so gossipy.
I haven't got the energy
to reply, to say how hurt
I'm feeling.
I feel so lonely.

I want to talk to someone.
But there's no one.
I can't tell Mom
or Dad.
I can't talk to my friends.
Or Benjamin.
I've lost Harriet.

I shove my phone
in my backpack
and go downstairs
for breakfast.

# Planetarium

Dad gives me a ride.
I sit in the passenger seat,
smoothing the envelope
on my lap
with my application in.

The summer internship feels
like the only thing
I have going for me
in the whole world.

We pull up outside.
There's a line already,
children and families
in broad daylight,
waiting to see
the night sky on the
domed ceiling inside.

"Good luck, Frank," says Dad
as I close the car door
and spot a group of girls
I think go to Thomas Jefferson.
They're staring at me.
Nudging. Whispering.

I look down,
but as I pass them,
one of them points at me.
I hear a muttered

"Period meme."
I hurry past
the rest of the line,
head down.

I go inside the cool atrium,
walk past the posters
reminding people
to look outside
at the blood moon
next week.

My heart thuds painfully
inside me.

I scan the room for Vidhi
to hand over
the envelope.
I spot her by the desk
near the solar system.
She glances up from her phone,
then stares at me.

"Oh," she says,
her mouth falling open.

                              "Hey," I say,
                    holding out my application.

But she doesn't take it.
She looks around
and says,
"Didn't you see
Elaine on your way in?"

"No," I say, checking behind me.
Elaine hasn't spoken to me
since she interviewed me.
I don't think she even
knows who I am.

"Right," Vidhi says,
fiddling with her rings,
then gets her walkie-talkie
and says, "Elaine could you come
to the first floor?"

She turns to me.
"Frankie," she says. "I'm sorry.
She should have phoned you."

"What is it?"
I try to read her face.

"Best to wait for Elaine."

We stand in awkward silence.
I slide the envelope
behind my back.
I wonder if I'm
about to get fired.

"Have I done
something wrong?"
I say, eventually.

Vidhi bites her bottom lip.
"Elaine doesn't think
you should be in today . . .

what with *everything online*."

"Oh," I say.
I don't know why,
but I thought
*that* stuff
wouldn't penetrate
this place.
Everything about it
seems so disconnected
from the internet.

Vidhi leans in and says,
"Sorry, I don't know
how she knows.
Her son's in high school.
I think maybe he showed
it to her."

My throat starts to close.
"You've seen?"

"Yes," she says.
"I'm sorry. I . . .
it's horrible."

I'm going to cry.
The closest exit
is just behind Vidhi.
I move toward it

just as Elaine comes
down the stairs.

"Frankie!" she says,

stopping me
at the open door.
"Good, Vidhi told you?
No hard feelings?
We'll get your shift covered
for a couple of weeks."

          I feel so stupid,
          my application
          behind my back.
          I have to get out of here.
          My chest trembles.

          My voice is weak,
          "Yeah," I say.
          "No, it's fine."

"We have quite a conservative
funding body . . .
and there are children,"
Elaine says, cocking her head
and wincing.
"Parents might complain
if they recognize *your face*.
It's just temporary."

Vidhi moves closer,
reaching out to touch
my arm again, but

          tears are coming,
          so I push the door
          and say in a hurry,
          "Honestly, it's fine,
          I understand.

                              Thanks anyway.
                               See you soon."

Vidhi says, "Have a nice day tod—"
but the door
clicks shut,
cutting her off.

# A Lonely Universe

I lean against the door
of the planetarium,
my hands shaking,
staring down at
cigarette stubs
on the ground,
my application
still in my hands.

Tears tumble off my cheeks
and splash onto brown paper,
making my name
an inky stain.
I feel so lonely.

My body presses
against the
planetarium door.
But the weight of it
pushes back at me
as though it's expelling me.

Inside that building,
the stars are all shining
neatly in their places.
An orderly twinkling
of constellations.

Ursa Major.
Ursa Minor.

Cassiopeia.
Pisces.
Pegasus.
Perseus.
Lyra.
Aries.
Hercules.

I'm on the other side.
I feel
so empty,
like even
the universe
has given up on me.

# Instead

I hide
in the trees
behind the car wash
clutching the brown envelope.

The smells of industrial soap
and wax waft over me
every few minutes
as I cry, on and off,
defiance fighting despair
inside me.

I take out my phone,
thinking about asking
Dad to pick me up early.
Maybe I'll say I'm sick . . .
      But there are
      so
      many
      notifications,
and I don't want to
see them but also
I can't help but read them.
I want to know
what's happening.

It starts to rain,
and I shuffle further
under the trees

hoping nobody sees me.
I'm pathetic,
hiding in the bushes,
shivering,
reading horrible comments
about me.

I'm actually
starting to feel sick.

My phone beeps
and I click on my texts,
hoping
there'll be, maybe,
a message from Harry

(She said
"You're nothing to me.")

or Benjamin.

But it's just low battery.

I wish he'd message me.
Or somehow contact me.

Maybe everything
would feel OK
if only he'd just admit
he told somebody.
Because he must have.
And now he's ghosting me.

Instead I get
sucked into

a long thread
that someone has tagged me in
where people are discussing
online shamings,
and how teenage girls
"are objectified sexually,"
and about "internet misogyny,"
        when my screen goes
                **black.**

        It's dead.

So now I can't even
call Dad, and instead
I wait under the tree
in the rain for the
remaining hour,
watching a blinking
digital clock
in a nearby car
until it's time
to go around the front
and be picked up.

When I get up,
I realize I'm still holding
the envelope
with my application in it.
It's soaking.

I shove it
into a nearby trash can

and dry my eyes,
preparing my lie
to explain why
I'm wet and shivering.

# Viral

"I think I'm coming
down with something,"
I tell Dad
as soon as I get in the car.
"My throat is sore."

"Oh, you poor thing,"
he says, feeling my forehead.
"Sorry I'm late.
I tried to call.
It went to voicemail."

"Battery," I mutter.

"Why didn't you wait inside?"

"Didn't want you
to have to get out
and find me."

Dad turns the heater on,
making the car
claustrophobically warm,
but at least he doesn't
ask me questions,
especially about handing in
my application.

Mom frowns

as I enter the hall
with Dad's arm around me.
"What happened?
Are you OK?"

                              "No." I sniff,
                         wriggling my feet
                     out of my wet shoes.
                        "I don't feel well."

"It was my fault," says Dad.
"I was late."

Mom reaches out to feel
my forehead too.
I don't know
what they glean
from doing this,
but it is comforting.
"You do feel warm.
Let's get you into bed."

                         I let her lead me
                   upstairs and tuck me in.
                    She brings me hot soup
                             and I eat it,
                         feeling like a fake,
                                   but

                             I am sick.
                          I've gone viral.

Shame has entered my bloodstream.

It's passed from digital me,
into reality, infecting
and poisoning
living me.

# DMs

I don't reply, but the girls still
message me directly,
saying they're here for me.

But it's not just them
DMing me.
On almost
all my socials,
complete strangers
are messaging me.

**Bethany**
Hey, gorgeous. We were
all just talking about you,
and wanted to say we're
thinking about you.
None of us agree
with what's happening.

> you ugly filthy ho
> you need to be stopped

**Marie**
Hey you. Thinking of you.
Hope you're OK?

> you slut bet you
> were gagging for it

**Leylah**

We're all going out tonight.
Wanna come? Might make
you feel better to get all
dressed up?

shiiiiit yo a hott piece o ass

They're going out?
With who?
With Harriet?
Do they really believe
that she didn't make the meme?
Who is she saying
it was?

I feel a bit fake,
but I copy and paste
exactly the same message
to all of them.

**Me**

Thanks, girls.
I'm actually sick,
so staying home.
Have fun tonight. X

**Leylah**

We'll miss your
pretty face, Frankie.

fml you're disgusting

**Marie**
Look after yourself.
Love you. X

you whore

**Bethany**
Just so you know,
Harriet's not coming.
She's not talking
to any of us
anymore.

bitch be diiiiiirty . . .

Maybe Harriet's
actually feeling guilty?

**And STILL,**
**even though**
**she must know**
**what's happening now,**
**she's not talking to me.**

Her silence says,
"You're nothing to me."

# Harriet

I wake up late
and lie in bed,
listening to Mom and Dad
empty the dishwasher
in the kitchen,
singing along to a song
on the radio,
like they don't have a care
in the world.

I wonder what the girls
did last night.
I wonder what Harriet did.
Who is she even hanging out with?
Maybe she's still grounded.

I check my phone
to see if there's anything
from the girls,
or Benjamin even,
but there's nothing
except the usual abuse.

I read it.
I'm *crushed* by it.
And I can't stop looking at it.

The thing that I don't get
is Harriet.

I trace my fingers across
the pattern of stars
on the case of my phone
and think about her being
angry enough with me
to actually
make
and post
that meme.

I thought I knew her.
I thought I understood her.
I know she can be mean,
but this mean?

I can't believe it.

And

            I can't believe
            how much it
            hurts.

# PEANUT BUTTER AND JELLY

No one's written
in the group for days,
but I can see Harriet's online,
and I've got nothing left
to lose, so I write:

                                        **Me**
                                  Hey girls,
                          how was last night?


**Leylah**
Ah it was so fun!
Hope you're managing to
ignore all the jerks online?
They're just assholes.

                    if my girl askd me to do
                       what you're into
                    I'd dump her skank ass

**Bethany**
We met some boys last night
from St. Matthew's,
and they were all saying
they knew about you
and thought it was horrible too.
Their school did an assembly
on online bullying, apparently.

Ignore the haters.
They can't harm you.

> @mazzymaz @gizmojim We found you
> @PhysicsFrankie HA. Tried to defend yourself.
> Pathetic bitch.

**Marie**
Yeah. It's so horrible.
We're all hoping it
blows over soon.

> she can suck me off

Then on the screen it says,

> **Harriet has left the group**

> Those tiny words
> are cold water
> engulfing my body.
> My heart is sinking.
> She can't say sorry.

**Bethany**
OMG. She can't leave!

> I'd love to do this to her

**Leylah**
She says she didn't
post the meme.
Maybe we should listen
to her?

## that just made me cum

**Bethany**
If she didn't do it,
why did she just leave
our group?

**Me**
Maybe she's not
talking to me.

**Bethany**
Don't worry. She's not
talking to anybody.

**Leylah**
I just think we should
listen to her if she says
it wasn't her.

**Bethany**
Erm . . . It was posted
ON HER PAGE???
Pretty hard to see how
it could not have been her.
She's always been kinda mean.
I don't believe her.

**Marie**
I feel bad to say it,
but I don't either.
That thing she said
about my period

was super shit of her.
She's out of control.

**Bethany**
Exactly. And that
pic she took of Frankie
in the shower.
She definitely made the meme.
It stinks of her.
She just doesn't know
how to say sorry.

lez find the bicth

**Marie**
How are you, Frankie?
We missed your face
last night.

download here to cum
on her stupid face

**Me**
I missed you guys too.
Glad you had fun.
Better go. XX

I can't talk about this anymore.
I click off the chat.

Then, thinking about Harriet,
I open my stargazing app
and see, above me,

on the other side of the ceiling,
the nearly full moon,
which will soon be
a blood moon.
But without Harriet,
I can't get excited about it.
Even thinking about it
makes me feel like shit.

# Digital Me

I stay in my room
almost all day.
Mom and Dad
keep popping in
to see if I'm OK
but there's a universe
between us
and I can't seem
to reach across
the abyss of this
online mess
to ask them
to help me.

# I Want to Stop Being

Nighttime comes.
I've been in bed
all day.
I feel disgusting,
but I can't stop reading,
scrolling,
checking
for more horrid things
being said about me.

I keep thinking
I should go to sleep,
and I'm really about to,
when I read something

that makes me fling
my phone
across the room.
It whacks the wall,
and I hear the impact
crack the screen.

I crawl
and pick it up again.

It doesn't make
any sense.
Why would someone
write these words?

I read it,
over and over,
scared,
because I don't
think they're joking.

My eyes
flood
until tears spill
onto the crackled
surface of my screen:

**Someone needs to rape you
you feminist bitch**

I can't stop shaking.
My insides are shrinking.
I want to stop being.

I stay completely still,
hoping
that
Mom
or Dad
come
soon
and check on me,
because
if they don't
I'm scared I might
turn into

*n o t h    i    n    g    . . .*

# SKIPPING

Monday morning
I lie in bed,
flat and gray,
an old sweater
with nothing left
to give.

Dad wants to
call the doctor,
but Mom persuades him
to leave me,
see how I feel
once I'm fully awake.

"Could Harriet

                  (the treacherous bitch)

stop by after school?"
Dad says.
"Or have you two
still not made up?"

            (I don't know if we ever will.
                Nothing to me.
                  Nothing.)

            "I'm fine," I say,

pulling the comforter
over my head.
"Just let me sleep."

"We'll call you later,"
Mom says.

"Or you call us," Dad adds.
"Or send us a text.
Anything."

I hear the front door close,
but I stay in bed,
wondering whether Harriet
will ever admit what she did.

And I think about Benjamin.
I wonder what he's doing.
I look at the photo he sent me,
back when everything
with him was dreamy.

Him in bed,
thinking about me.
I feel so stupid,
believing he liked me.
He hasn't even messaged me.

At ten o'clock I get up,
unsteady on my feet,
and go to the living room,
sit down, and cradle
my broken phone

to find out
what's happening
to me now.

I turn on the TV for company
and pull a blanket up for safety,
and I start to read.
I thought it would be
fading by now.
But it's getting worse
somehow.

I have a DM from
someone I don't know
called TheDonaldoBro.
I have so many messages
I haven't even tried
to read them all,
but I see the start of this one:

I'm going to find out where you live . . .

so I click
to read the rest

and I'm going to come
and rape you to teach you a lesson,
you filthy little cunt.

# (No title)

my
blood
runs
cold

my hands
are       wet
i
cannot
      see

my mouth    fills
with
spit
my   throat is dry
i'm gonna    puke
i want to die

      i want to
leave the internet

take             myself
back
but      i know  it's
too late        for that

# KNOCK, KNOCK

I stare at my phone.
I'm going to find out where you live
Vomit creeps up my throat,
but then—

KNOCK, KNOCK.

Someone is at our door.
My arms are shaking.

KNOCK, KNOCK.

What should I do?
Call the police?
Hide?
Weep?

I sweat
and creep
to the window
and peep.

A man
is standing
in our front yard—

KNOCK, KNOCK.

He turns his head
and looks right at me

through the window.
He can see me.

My heart
explodes.

Then he waves
a brown box at me.
Mouths *"Delivery."*

I go to the door
and shout,
"Leave it outside!"

"Need a signature, honey."
The man's voice
is loud inside.

"Please!" I add.
I sound pathetic.

"No can do," he says.

Isn't this
what someone would say
if they were trying
to trick me to let them inside?

I take a deep breath,
shout, "Go away!"
Then I sit on the floor
under the window
and listen, waiting
to hear him leave.

The mail slot clatters,
and his voice comes inside.
"Hello?" he calls.
"You still inside?
Are you OK?"

                                    I start to cry.
                                    "GO AWAY!"
                                    I shout.
                      "LEAVE ME ALONE,
           OR I'LL CALL THE POLICE!"

I hear the mail slot close
and his voice mutter,
"All right, all right."

Then I hear
him knocking on
Harriet's door.
I hear Lola answer.

"Sure, I'll sign for it."

Then I hear him say,
"Thanks, gorgeous,"
and the sound of his
footsteps fades up the path.

Just a delivery guy.

                                  I feel ridiculous.
                      Lola is a few feet away,
                         but I'm sitting here,
                       sobbing and shaking.

I can't even talk to her,
because this is all
her daughter's fault

and I'm scared
to go outside.

# The Walking Dead

I want my life back.
I want to go outside
and be nobody again:
Just a girl, going to school.
Just a girl, doing gym.
Just a girl, walking
with her best friend
to get croissants
to eat in her tree house
before dawn.

Just a girl,
looking up at the night sky,
wondering how we got here
and sighing at
the marvel of life.

I miss my life.
I miss my best friend.

I'm alive.
Yet not alive.
I am the walking dead.

# PART THREE

# Busted

On Tuesday morning,
my parents decide
my virus has sufficiently
subsided
and I'll survive
a day in school.

I try to persuade them
to let me stay home,
but I don't have a fever,
and I can't tell the truth,

so I leave the house
and hide in the alley,
for just enough time
for Dad and Mom
to go to work.
Then I scurry home.

But when I open
the front door
Mom is right there.

"Frankie. What's going on?"
Her face is calm,
but this is what it does
before the storm.

I reach for a lie:
"I forgot my gym clothes."

But she holds up her iPad,
and on it I see
there's an email from school.
"Then why is Mr. Adamson
asking me and Dad
to come in for a meeting
tomorrow afternoon?"

"I don't know," I say,
my insides squirming,
attempting to
escape my body.

Mom says,
"You weren't going in today.
And you didn't finish on Friday.
And what about yesterday?
Were you actually sick?
I want you to stop lying."

*I* want to stop lying,
but how can I tell her
what's happening to me
because
I was horny
and on my period
and a dirty slu—

"Frankie!" she says.
"Whatever it is,
you can tell me."

I shake my head.
I *can't* tell her this.
I cannot bear for her to know
I got fing—

"You can tell me anything.
You're my own
flesh and blood."

Then I notice
there are tears in *her* eyes.

Why is *she* crying?

"I can't tell you, Mom . . ." I say.
But even as I hear my words
f l o a t   h e r   w a y,
my hand goes
to my shattered phone,
and I open the page
*Freaky Frankie Finger Fun.*
She's going to find out anyway.
I hand my phone to Mom
and turn away.

I can't watch her face
as she sees
all the comments
and pictures
and memes
about me.

But I can't not watch her face
and wonder

which post she is on:

The original meme
    about the period
    fingering?

Or maybe some of the
Photoshopped images
where disgusting things
have been done
to the fingers
and to my face.

Then Mom breathes out very loud.
"WHAT IS THIS?" she practically yells.

                I've never seen her face like this:
                    her nostrils flared,
                        her skin tight,
                            white
                            like bone.

                        But I can't speak.
                    I don't have the words
                        to explain what *it* is.

Mom stares at me
so long I wonder if she'll ever speak,
and all I can think is:
        how is she
        going to love me
        after this?

Even my blood
feels cold in my veins,
like it doesn't want to be
part of my shame.

I close my eyes
and look at the dark,
and start to drift apart.

But then I feel Mom's arms
close across me,
wrapping around
my trembling body,
squeezing me.

I press my head
against her chest,
so close and still
I can hear her heartbeat,
and I let go.

She holds me tightly
as though she's
trying to say:
*I can hold you together.*

But she must know
she can't.

# Family Meeting

Eventually
I stop sobbing,
and she lets go of me
and gets out her phone.

                         "Mom!
                What are you doing?"
        I ask, following her to the kitchen.

"I'm calling Dad."

                      "Why?"

"To ask him to come home.
He needs to see this."

                   "Mom! No.
          Please don't show Da—"

But he's already answered,
and Mom's saying,
"Hello, it's me. Do you mind
coming home at lunch today?
. . .
Now is even better.
. . .
      That's great.
      . . .
         See you in five."

"Mom! Send me to my room.
Take my phone away.
Ground me.
Just don't tell Dad.
Please."

"That's not fair, Frankie.
How is he supposed to
understand you,
to support you,
if you keep things
from him?"

And there I was,
thinking the humiliation
had peaked.

Dad comes home
and walks into the kitchen,
looking worried.

I can't cope with the embarrassment,
so I go to the table and sit down
with my head in my hands,
and listen to Mom explaining
what he's about to see.

I can tell when he's scrolling
by the sounds of his breathing.
I wonder what he's reading,
what he's seeing,
and then I hear sniffling.

I lift my head.
"Oh, Dad!" I say.
"Please, don't cry."

"Why would anyone do this?"
he says, wiping his eyes.

I'm not sure what he means by *this*.
What I did?
Or what's been done to me?

And then I wonder
if my parents
have gotten an email
from Mr. Adamson, maybe
Harriet's mom has one too.

I wonder if Harriet
will tell her the truth,
or just pretend
she's innocent.

"Why you?" he says.

"Why anyone, Dad?" I say.
*He's* supposed to be comforting me.
"It's just jerks online,
not thinking about
the real life behind
what they're doing."
(And my ex–best friend
leaking my secrets to be mean.)

"But why would so many people

make up all this stuff about *you*?"

(Because I'm disgusting.)
I shrug.
"It's not all made up."

"What do you mean?"

"The meme at the top.
That's sort of true."

"What's a meme?" says Mom.

"A picture with words,
like captions, on it," I say,
my skin prickling
as I start sweating.

Dad scrolls on my phone
then turns it to face me,
"You mean this one?"
He's showing me
the one that says,
"I got fingered on my period
and I bloody loved it."

"That's the one,"
I say as a
gravitational wave of
embarrassment travels through me,
warping me.

Mom looks around to see.
"Yes, the period thing.

Well, that's nothing
to be ashamed of.
It's only blood.
Gosh, the internet
is sexist."

But Dad's gone pale,
and I wait,
watching his face,
as he comes over
and hugs me,
but he doesn't
actually look at me.

"We need to get this
taken down,"
Dad says.

                              "Dad," I say. "It's all over
                                            the internet.
                                  You can't delete it."

"Then we'll call the police,"
he says into his hands,

                                    not looking at me.

                          He hasn't looked at me
                          since he saw the meme.

"We need to report it."

                                  I feel so dirty
                          hearing those words.
                          This is so unfair.

"Yes," says Mom.
"I agree.
We have to call
the police.
Maybe after we've seen
Mr. Adamson."

                              I knew
                         they'd say this.
                       I've looked it up.
                "There's basically nothing
                    the police can do."

"We'll still report it,"
Dad sighs
and runs his hands
down his face.

                              And I say,
                         "I'm sorry. This
                       is all my fault."

"No!" Mom says.
"You haven't done
anything wrong,
have you?"

                       "No." I shake my head.
                       And try to believe it.

"This is not your fault,"
she says, coming over
and holding me.

I let her squeeze me
and don't try to see
what Dad's doing.
What he's thinking.

"We're not going to sit back
and do nothing. We're going
to put this right."

I wish Dad would say
something reassuring
so I know he still accepts me,
still loves me.

Mom lets go of me,
and I look at Dad
and say, "Are you mad at me?"
My voice is shaky.

"Of course not," says Dad,
shaking his head.

But I don't believe him.

He stands up
and goes to the sink
and with his back
to me he says,
"You were going to tell me
if you had a boyfriend."

I pause, then say,
"He's not my boyfriend."

Oh god.
What must he think of me
that I'd do something
so intimate
with just *anybody*?

It all suddenly seems so dirty.
It really wasn't supposed to be.

Mom takes my hand.
"Did *he* do this viral thing?"

"No. And it takes more
than one person
to make something
go viral."

"We do know that," says Mom.
"But did one of you tell someone?"

"I didn't tell anyone."

"We could talk to his parents!"
Dad says, turning around.

"What's that
going to achieve?"
I'm so angry with Benjamin
for blabbing to everyone,
but my parents
talking to his parents
about *this*?
#NoWay

"Please," says Dad,
"just tell us his name."
As if knowing something
will anchor him.

"Benjamin." I sigh.
"His name is Benjamin.
But he didn't make the meme."

"Then who did?"

I hesitate,
then say,
"I don't know who,
but the damage is done."

What would they do
if they knew it was
Harriet who brought
all this on me?

"You're right," says Mom, nodding.
"The important thing
is you going back
to school."

"Not today!" I say.

Mom looks at her watch.
"It'll be lunchtime shortly."
Then she looks at Dad.
They nod at each other,
agreeing at least
to this tiniest mercy—
to let me continue hiding

for one more afternoon.

"You can stay home today," she says.
"But tomorrow, you go in.
And we'll talk to the principal
in this meeting."

Dad nods
but goes to leave the kitchen.
"I'm sorry, Frankie.
I need some space to think."

                              "Dad!" I say.
                         "What are you doing?"

"Just give him a moment."

                              "Oh god," I say.
                    "He's going to look up Benjamin."

"No," says Mom firmly.
"He wouldn't do that."

                         I feel my chest tightening
                         as Dad's footsteps fade.
                         He can't even look at me.
                              "He's ashamed of me."

"He's not," she says.

                                   But only
                         to make me feel better.
                         "I really don't want
                         to go to school tomorrow."

"You can do this.
You're strong.
And we'll be there
in the afternoon
to support you."

                              Ugh.
              My *parents* are going to come in.
          Everyone is going to know they know.
                        Everything.

                    "This is going to be
                      so embarrassing.
              Please don't make me go."

"You can do this,"
Mom says, crouching
in front of me and
holding my arms,
reassuringly.
"Are you ashamed?"

                          I think about it.
                              I mean
                              I really
                              think
                          about it.

                        Am I ashamed?
              I think back to that afternoon.
                    To me and Benjamin
                          stargazing,
                            talking,

and me getting my period
on his fingers.

It was embarrassing,
but not shameful.
The shame has come from
what other people have said.
I can't do
anything about them.

I would do it again.

I shake my head.
"No," I say, "I'm not ashamed."
And as I say it
I feel *fast* and
f r e e
like a particle
that's just been
fired around the Large Hadron Collider.

I feel like me.

I pick up my phone,
instinctively,

but Mom gently
pries it out of my hands.
"I'd better keep this,"
she says, pocketing it,
"Just until we've
worked out how to
get this taken down."

# Doing Something

Mom tells me she's going
to check on Dad, and
I don't mind.
My thoughts are racing.

I make myself a sandwich
and eat it in the kitchen,
chewing it slowly,
trying to think clearly.

I can't hear my parents
speaking, or even moving.
The house is so silent,
incongruous with
my noisy, defiant thinking.

I don't want to retreat
back to my room,
I'm raring to go,
to do something.

I clear up my lunch
and then sit in the kitchen
listening to the tap dripping,
trying not to think of
Dad being ashamed of me,
even if Mom says he isn't.

I jiggle my leg
until I can't bear it,

and I stand up,
go to the door,
pull on my sneakers,
and shout,
"I'm going out!"

I surprise myself
as I open the front door
and step outside
into the wide world.

I've got time to kill
before school is out,
so I walk away from home
and take a long route
around the houses,
thinking about
what I've gone through,
how much I've been alone,
how impotent it's made me feel.

I know I'm lucky
to have Mom and Dad,
but they can't sort this out.
Their only plan
is to try to take stuff down.
They have no clue.

I think about
the waitress in the bathroom
that night, who told me
I should say something.
I've been scared to speak
to anybody since it blew up online.

I keep checking the time,
then finally
at three
I turn sharply
and walk quickly
down the street.
I can talk to Benjamin.

I can confront him again.

Now that I think about it,
time has given me clarity,
and even though I know
he didn't make the meme,
I do know he told somebody.

It's easy really,
      one turn here,
            down the next street,
      along a few more,
      and before I know it
I'm looking at his
red front door.

I don't let myself think.
I don't let myself stop.
I just walk up to it,
reach out with my fist,
and knock on it.

# Fix It

I stand still and wait,
braced to deliver
my scathing reproach.
I watch his shadow approach
through the cloudy glass,
and then

Benjamin's mom
opens the door,
and I'm totally thrown.

"Hello," she says, smiling.

> "Er . . . hi," I say, searching
> for words to explain
> who I am
> and what I'm doing
> standing here
> looking determined.
> "I'm . . . er . . .
> is . . . er . . .
> Benjamin in?"
> I finally get out.

She tilts her head,
gives a flicker of a grin,
before standing aside
and saying,
"Sure, come in."

My eyes fall straight
on Benjamin's sneakers
lying on the floor at
the foot of the stairs.
The same ones he
took off in my front hall
right before we got
almost completely naked.

"Go on up,"
she says, pointing
to a door at the top
of the stairs.
"He's in his room."

"Thanks," I mutter,
slipping off my shoes,
the carpet squashing softly
beneath my bare feet.

I climb the stairs,
wondering if my parents
would ever be so cool
about letting a boy
come up to my room.

But before I'm at the top,
Benjamin's mom shouts up,
"Someone's here for you!
Keep the door open!"

And I'm in his doorway,
breathing in the clean,
toasty-sweet

smell of his room.

Benjamin is lying
on his bed.
"OK!" he shouts
down to his mom,
not looking up
from his laptop,
which is on the bed
next to him.

His rugby uniform is on the floor,
and on the wall above his head
is a huge poster
of what I know to be
a Cassini-mission photo
of Saturn's icy rings.

Benjamin taps the keys

and I look at his screen

and I **freeze.**

Half of the meme
fills his screen.
Not the picture of me,
but the one that's always
next to me, with the
bloodied fingers.
A stranger's fingers.

Why is he looking
at that bit on its own?

I feel **DISGUSTING.**

> A whimper escapes me.

Benjamin turns
and practically
falls off his bed
as he sees me,
and scrambles up.

"Frankie!" he says.
"What are you do—"

> "What are *you* doing?"
> I say, pointing at his screen.
> I try to sound strong.
> I feel so small.
> I wish I hadn't come.
> I want to fall
> into a black hole.

Benjamin looks from
me to his screen.
Panicking.
Guilty.

> I'm so confused.
> I know, *know*,
> he told someone,
> but . . .
> "Did you have something
> to do with the me—"

"No!" he says, shaking his head.

"I'm trying to help you!"

                    I search his face,
                  wondering how he
            could possibly be helping me.

"I can't believe you're here,"
he says, taking a step
closer to me. Then stopping.
"Can I show you
something I've just
found out? It's amazing."

He pulls the laptop
to the edge of the bed,
kneels on the floor,
and starts clicking.

                    I move a little closer,
                watching over his shoulder,
              curiosity silencing my anger.

Then he brings up
reams of white text
against a black screen.

"The metadata
shows where
the fingers photo
was taken."

                              "It's geotagged?"

"Exactly," Benjamin says,

his eyes wide and hopeful.
"This is not a stock photo.
It was taken just before
the meme was posted.
At about one a.m. that morning.
            Locally.
But it was nowhere
near Harriet's house."

                    "Then where?!" I say,
                        my heart lifting,
                            skipping,
        as I try to stop myself from imagining
                    what it would mean
                        if the meme
                            wasn't
                            Harriet's.

"There's only one person
I know who lives
in the area where the
photo was taken."
Benjamin pauses.
He looks worried.
"Jackson."

                            I blink.
                And shake my head,
                    scared to catch up
                    with what he's said,
            because of what it means.

            Did Harriet really not make the meme?
                "So . . ." I say, swallowing.

"Are you saying
Jackson made the meme?"

Benjamin nods

and
I realize I'm standing,
guilt and regret
battling in my guts.
"Harriet hasn't been lying."

"She could have
been with him."

"No," I say, shaking my head.
"She was grounded."
I bend over, feeling
almost sick with relief.
I breathe out deeply.
Then breathe in,
trying to take it all in.

I was so angry with her
about the shower photo,
I believed she'd do *anything* mean.
Even the meme.

But at the same time as I'm
realizing Harriet
didn't make the meme,
I'm realizing that
Benjamin still blabbed
to somebody.
He was the only one
who knew.

"You told Jackson!"
I say, standing up straight
to look at Benjamin.

"I didn't!" he says.

"Stop lying!" I say,
my voice rising,
hoping his mom
doesn't hear me.

"It was posted on *her* page.
How did he get into
her account if she
wasn't there?"

"Maybe he guessed it?"
I say, thinking about how
all her passwords are
variations of Oreo,

and how she was salivating
over her milkshake
in front of him
when we went ice skating,

and how Jackson knew
her phone's passcode
was 0000.

"You don't need to know why,
but her password would have
been really easy
for him to figure out."

"But that doesn't mean he—"

"Just admit you told
Jackson what we did!"
I snap.
I need to go
and see Harriet.

"I didn't," he says.

"Stop ly—"

"Wait!" he says, pleading,
his hands on his head,
compressing his curls,
as though he's trying
to force something out.

"I told my sister.
I texted her
when I got home
that afternoon.
I was worried I'd hurt you."

"You told your sister?"
I ask, incredulous.

Benjamin nods.
"I didn't know what else to do.
She works weird hours
in California so
she didn't reply
until the next morning.
I was in school.

I think Jackson read
the message I sent my sister
over my shoulder."

I stare at Benjamin,
searching his face
to see if he's lying.
Can that really be it?
Something so naive?
So innocent?

"I'm sorry.
I should have told you.
I just hoped so much
it wasn't all my fault.
My sister's been helping me
take the worst stuff down."

My temper is rising again.
"That's what my parents
said we should do
when they found out."

"Your parents *know*?"

"They know everything.
They're coming in to
see Mr. Adamson tomorrow.

Why didn't you just tell me?"
I'm almost shouting.

Benjamin sighs.
"I'm really sorry.

I couldn't bear it.
I was just pretending
it wasn't my fault.
I felt terrible."

"*You* felt terrible?"
I am shouting now.

"Everything OK?"
Benjamin's mom calls
up the stairs.

"Yes!" he calls back. "Fine!"

But I'm not fine.
I'm furious.
"And you ignored me!"

"My parents have
my phone."

"There are other ways
to contact me,"
I say, nodding at his laptop.

"You're right," he says.
"I just wanted to
fix it for you,
then show you."

I shake my head.
"I didn't need you
to fix it for me.
I just wanted you

to be there for me."

Benjamin looks
genuinely surprised.
"Is that all?"

"That's all."

Benjamin swallows.
His Adam's apple bobs
at the neck of his T-shirt.
"I felt so guilty.
I'm sorry.
I was hiding."

"You were lying."

Benjamin nods.
"I wish I'd just told
you the truth.
I was lying to myself too.
I didn't know what to do.
I really like you."

"I like you too.
But I don't trust you."

Benjamin looks down at his feet,
then up at me.
"Maybe over time
I can gain that back?"
Benjamin says.

"I really hope we can
hang out again."

"I hope so too," I say.
Maybe he was
just ashamed like me.
But I need
time to think.
"Send me that thing,"
I say, pointing
to his screen
as I leave.

I have an idea forming, but
before I do anything
I have to talk to Harriet.

# An Apology

I run all the way
from Benjamin's house
my legs working
as hard as my brain
straining to sort
the muddling feelings
of guilt
from shame.

I reach Harriet's house,
legs aching,
heart pounding,
mouth bursting with
an apology I desperately
hope isn't too late.

Harriet opens her front door
and takes a step back
as she sees it's me.

Her face is red.
Her eyes are puffy.

"Frankie," she says.
"What's happening?"

Sweat is trickling
down my spine
and I'm panting from running
as I blurt out,

"I know you didn't
make the meme."

I stop to breathe,
my throat tightening.

"Jackson hacked you.
Benjamin can prove it."

I lean over
and gasp for breath,
then stand back up
and search her face.

Hoping she understands
what I'm saying.

Hoping she won't slam
the door in my face.

Her brow furrows.
She blinks slowly.
Sniffs a little.
"No one believed me."

"We were so angry."

She starts nodding,
sobbing, and saying,
"It wasn't me," over and over
as though she's making up
for all the time she's been
coping with everyone
thinking it was her.

"Harry," I say,
reaching out to her.
"I'm so sorry."

She looks at me
with her bloodshot eyes,
sniffs loudly, and says,
"I did some horrible things,
but I would never do
something so cruel."

"I know," I say, swallowing,
my heart hurting from
seeing how much
pain Harriet's in.
"I'm sorry I didn't believe you."
Tears slide
down my hot cheeks.
"I wanted to,
but it was so convincing.
And I was so angry at you."

Harriet nods,
tears still pouring
down her cheeks too.
"You had every right to be."

"Please forgive me?"

"*Me* forgive *you*?"
Harriet says, wiping
her nose on her sleeve.
"Frankie, I was awful to you.
I took that shower photo.

I pushed you down.
I snapped over
that whole email thing.
It was so embarrassing.
I wanted to get you into
as much trouble as me.
I'm the one who
should be saying
sorry to you."

"What I said to you in the bathroom
that day was horrible."

"It was pretty mean."

"I just didn't understand
why you'd send
a picture like that."

"I think in my
sleep-addled state, I
thought it would make
Mr. B like me as much
as he likes you.
I'm not as smart as you."

"Oh, Harry. You are so smart," I say.
"I am the idiot.
I shouldn't have judged you
about the email.
I should have just
been there for you."

Harriet winces.

"I should have
been there for *you*.
I didn't know
how to come back to you."

                              "I didn't, either.
                              But I am so, so sorry."

                         The afternoon breeze
                         sweeps the clouds aside
                         and a sunbeam falls on us,
                         illuminating us, ridiculously,
                              both crying messily,
                         standing on the doorstep,
                         tears dripping from our faces.

"I'm more sorry
than I can ever say.
To the moon and back
or something really big
and cheesy like that.
You're not nothing to me.
You're *everything*."

                              "God, I've missed you!"

"I've missed you too."

                         Then we hug each other,
                              squeezing tightly,
                              sort of laughing,
                              sort of crying,
                         and for the first time in forever
                         I feel like laughing.

So I say,
"My parents saw
my porno debut,"
and I watch her

as her eyes go so wide
they look like they're
going to fall out of her face.

# An Idea

"OMG, tell me
everything
immediately!"

                    "I showed them *everything.*"

"Everything everything?"

                    "Everything everything.
                            Pirate porn.
                          The *Carrie* one.
                           The vampire
                    with the strap-on."

"You didn't edit?"
Harriet says, covering her face.

                            "I couldn't edit!
                  It's on the frickin' internet."

"Shi-i-it," she says,
her hands on her face.
"What did they say?"

                    "Well, they took my phone
                            for a start."

"No!" Harriet gasps.
"It wasn't *your* fault."

"I know!" I say.
"And they have to come
for a meeting tomorrow
with Mr. Adamson."

"And my mom too," she says.
"I guess someone told Mr. Adamson
about it being on my page first."

"That's not fair though!
You didn't do it."

"At least now I can prove it."

"About that," I say.
"I have an idea."

"Tell me!" says Harriet.
"I'm all ears."

# Grabbing the Bull

I wake at dawn,
dread coiled
thickly in my guts
like a wet snake.

I used to be
a *good girl,*
but what does that even mean?

Today,
I *might* get expelled
for what we have planned,
but I'm going to
see this through;
we have a plan,
and I want to
reclaim the truth.

It's laugh or be laughed at.
Kill or be killed.

I get up,
my legs heavy,
reluctant to carry me
even to the bathroom.

I sit on the toilet,
my stomach writhing,
trying to keep me
from heading outside.

But I'm going to school
today. I just have
to stick to the plan.

I get ready like normal,
and put everything
I need inside my backpack
out of my parents' sight.

I don't tell them
what Harriet
and the girls
and I
planned last night.
There's no point
winding them up,
or having them
try to stop me.
They don't have the answers.

"Ready?" says Mom.

I nod.

"Good for you, Frank,"
Dad says,

and maybe I'm imagining it,

but I'm sure he's still
being weird with me.

I just want him to not
be ashamed of me.

"Be brave," says Mom.
"Fighting problems head-on
can make them melt away.
Grab the bull by the horns."

I'll try.
But there's every chance
I'll end up getting
trampled on today.

"I'm so proud of you,"
Mom says.

I know she is *now*.
I'm just not sure if our plan
is exactly what she's
got in mind.

# Reclaiming My Reputation

Harriet and I hide
around the corner
from the entrance
to the assembly
while our class
files inside.

               "Do you feel OK
        about seeing Jackson?"

Harriet nods.
"I'm not thinking about him.
I'm thinking about
Benjamin texting his sister
for sex advice!"

Then we hear a fake cough.
"That's the signal from Marie.
Everyone is in assembly.
Ready?"

She opens her backpack,
and hands me my T-shirt.
"I've got mine on.
Put your hoodie on
over the top."

               I nod and do it,

                      but my guts coil up.

She squeezes my hand.
"You are brave,"
she says.

               And when I think about
               what I've been through,
                    I realize I am.

We get up
and walk around the corner
of the building.
A group of girls
from the year above
walk past us, pointing
and whispering,
(. . . on her *period*).

Yesterday, that might have
broken me,
but today it seems to
bounce off me.
I won't be shamed
for getting my period.
It's only blood.

Outside the auditorium
Marie is holding an empty
marker pen box
and two paper bags
that flutter in the breeze.

"They've all been taken!"

she says, excitedly.
"Almost everyone took one.
The printed ones
and the blank ones."

Then Marie grabs me,
hugs me.
"Leylah's inside already."

Then Harriet says,
"Look! Mr. Adamson
is coming!"
And we turn to see
Bethany walking with him,
keeping him distracted.

We scurry in
and slip behind
the long black curtain
that hangs across the stage.

Harriet peeks through the gap,

        but in the muffled noise
          behind the curtain
            in the dark,
             I feel uncertain.

             But I remember,
             Newton's third law.
       *For every action*
      *there is an equal and*
      *opposite reaction.*

     This is ours.

"You can do this,"
Harriet says, grinning.
"I'll be in the sound booth,"
she says, pointing up at the
back of the auditorium.

Then she turns
and leaves.

I wait,
and just
breathe,
and it feels
as though
time
slows,
warped
by the mass
of what we're
about to do.

Then all the auditorium lights
go off, and I count to three,
then throw myself through
the curtain, into the darkness.

I can see a sliver
of green emergency light
reflecting off Mr. Adamson's head
at the side.
He's waiting offstage,
and next to him is
Bethany, who has
hopefully persuaded him

to give us a few minutes.
Then Harriet
flips the spotlight on,
lighting the banner behind me.

# THIS ASSEMBLY IS
# A #NoShame ZONE

And in front of it,
      I am bathed in
         bright
            white
               incandescent
                   light
     choosing to be seen.
       The real me.

     I've spent
        so much time
          alone online
             hiding from the world
               in the silence of
          my room,
            I could never have imagined
       how comforting
    the gentle rustle
    of a crowd of people
could be.

I think about my friends
helping me to organize this.
About Marie nabbing
a box of plain T-shirts
from her dad's business

347

and the five of us giggling
and scribbling with markers
up in the tree house
until early this morning.

And I think about Harriet
up in the booth now,
supporting me.

I take a deep breath.
I hear the room wait
for me to say
what I need to say.

Finally I speak:
"I got publicly shamed.
What happened to me
was a nightmare.
I hid and I felt ashamed.
But what did I actually do?"

The noise lifts, then falls from chatter
       to mutters
              to silence
                    as they watch me
                          take off my hoodie.

            On my T-shirt,
              printed out
            and ironed on,
              is the meme.

              Only . . .

I've crossed out
some words.

# I GOT ~~FINGERED ON~~ MY PERIOD ~~AND I BLOODY LOVED IT~~

My whole year
cheers, and I turn around
so they can read the back:

# IT'S ONLY BLOOD
## #NoShame

And I get to watch
Mr. Adamson's face
as he reads the front,
and his eyebrows go up
but he starts nodding,
like he approves of
what he's reading.

Then Harriet throws
more spotlights on,
lighting up
Leylah,

Bethany,

and

Marie,
who are joining me, onstage.

Their shirts say
**I GET MY PERIOD TOO.**
**IT'S ONLY BLOOD**
**#NoShame**

I bite my lip to stop the grin
as Harriet lights
the whole auditorium,
and I see
it's not just my friends.
Lots of the girls
are wearing them.
They stand in unison,
and I read the rows of shirts
in the auditorium,
saying
over
      and over
           and over
                again


IT'S ONLY BLOOD #NoShame IT'S ONLY
BLOOD #NoShame IT'S ONLY BLOOD
#NoShame IT'S ONLY BLOOD #NoShame
IT'S ONLY BLOOD #NoShame IT'S ONLY
BLOOD #NoShame IT'S ONLY BLOOD
#NoShame IT'S ONLY BLOOD #NoShame
IT'S ONLY BLOOD #NoShame IT'S ONLY
BLOOD #NoShame IT'S ONLY BLOOD
#NoShame IT'S ONLY BLOOD #NoShame
IT'S ONLY BLOOD #NoShame IT'S ONLY
BLOOD #NoShame IT'S ONLY BLOOD

And it was.

It was only blood.

Then I notice
that a few people
have made their
own #NoShame T-shirts
and have put them on
over their clothes.

Jasmine's says
**I'm still a Belieber.**
**#NoShame**

Lee's says
**I thought a blow job**
**meant you blow on it.**
**#NoShame**

Dev's says
**I pick my nose**
**and eat it.**
**#NoShame**

Charlie's says
**I once accidentally**
**ate dog food.**
**#NoShame**

then Michael Li
takes off his hoodie.
His T-shirt says
**I'm gay.**
**#NoShame**
and a few people laugh

because he's been out
since at least elementary school.

I scan the crowd for Benjamin.
I find him.
He's crouching,
writing something
on a shirt.

He pulls it on
and it takes a moment
for everyone to realize
there's a new one.

**I asked my sister**
**if it was OK**
**to finger my girlfriend**
**on her period.**
**#NoShame**

Benjamin raises his eyebrows,
like he's checking to see
if it's OK with me
that he called me
his girlfriend.

I melt a bit
and smile at him,
nodding.

And Benjamin grins at me.

Harriet walks onto the stage
to stand beside me

"Oh my god,"
she whispers.
"Benjamin's T-shirt!
*Embarrassing.*"

But then she adds,
"He's very sweet."

She pulls off
her own sweater.
Her floral shampoo smell
surrounds me,
which only makes it funnier
when I look down
and read her T-shirt:

**I pooped
on the floor
in assembly
in second grade.
#NoShame**

I think I would read a thousand
abusive DMs for just *one*
assembly like this
where we're all
laughing together.

It's not as if by
being open all
the shame goes away,
but laughing about it
somehow seems
to take some of its

power away.

And right now,
I don't feel even slightly
ashamed.
I just feel
#Happy.

I glance over at Mr. Adamson,
clapping along with everyone.
He looks at me,
and he directs his applause
at me, nodding and smiling.

Everyone is
whooping
and cheering
with their phones out,
filming,
and Harriet puts
her arm around me
and I squish her to me,
feeling her warmth
spread over me:
a thermic reaction,
generating laughter,
instead of friction.

Then Harriet whispers to me,
"Should I do it now?"

And I look at Mr. Adamson,
to check he's watching.

He's still clapping,
nodding,
loving the student-led
initiative
we're showing.

          I nod, my stomach wriggling.

"And one more thing,"
Harriet shouts
toward Mr. Adamson.

Then she points at Jackson
and says, "He made the meme."

          I don't want to
          humiliate Jackson
          (I sort of do)
          but I do want something
          to happen to him.
          I want him to be made
          to understand.

"Shut up!" shouts Jackson.
"It wasn't me."

"You know it was," she says.

"Prove it!" he snarls,
looking to Dev for solidarity.
But Dev shakes his head
and moves
a little away.

Then Harriet peels off
her T-shirt,
revealing another one
underneath.

**These are Jackson
Twigger's Fingers
#HeMadeTheMeme**

Then she turns around
to show the back,
where she's printed the evidence.
  The GPS location
  from the finger picture
  showing it was taken
  at Jackson's address.

"Oh, fuck off," shouts Jackson.
"Everyone shared it—"

"JACKSON TWIGGER!"
bellows Mr. Adamson,
making Jackson jump.
"This is not funny.
You will come with me
immediately after assembly.
If you did
what they say you did,
this will be taken
very
very
seriously."

# After Assembly

Everyone files out of
assembly chatting excitedly,
and some come over
to tell us how much
what we just did
meant to them.

I look at my friends
as we stand in a circle:
the five of us united
by the power of
telling the story again,
in our own words.

"Good job, all of you,"
says Mr. B, beaming.
"Periods are just biology."
But he goes a bit red

and I try not to catch
anyone's eye,
because I can feel
the whole group
resisting the urge
to start giggling,
which would totally spoil
our whole point.

But Marie saves us all,
saying, "Thanks, sir."

Then Mr. B says,
"Frankie"—and his tone
changes as he speaks earnestly—
"what you did in there
was really brave.
It might not be obvious,
but bravery is something
every good scientist needs."

"Thank you, sir," I say.
And I mean it.
I think I'm going to cry.

"Your essay was terrific.
Let me know what the
planetarium says, won't you?"

"Yes, sir," I say,
nodding and remembering
my soggy application.

"And keep ignoring
those idiots online,"
he adds, going back
to the usual jokey Mr. B.
"Remember: the universe
is made of
protons, neutrons, electrons,
and morons. Ha ha."
Then he walks away,
still laughing at his own joke.

I bite my lip, then turn
to Harriet and whisper,

"I threw my
application away."

"What?" she says,
looking horrified.

"The deadline is today.
Did you get yours in?"

"I'm not applying."

"Why not?" I say.

"Because my heart isn't in it.
I don't really want it.
I'm going for this
photography thing instead.
But you *have to* apply.
Do you still have your essay?"

"It's all in my email,"
I say, mentally checking
the bits I'll need
to send to Vidhi.

"Then, let's go!" she says.
"Do it now while you're on
a winning streak!"

"OK!" I say, "but maybe
they won't want me."

"Of course they will!"
says Harriet as she grabs me and drags me

toward the computer lab.

It's amazing how uplifting
and empowering
having my best friend
beside me can be.

# Normal Girls

At the end of the day,
after the longest meeting,
where Mr. Adamson
gave us time
and space to explain
to Jackson
what he actually did to me,
and to Harriet too,
and to all the girls
to some extent,
we're finally free.

We follow
our parents out
of Mr. Adamson's office,
Jackson and his parents
right behind us.

We turn one way,
and his family turns the other.
We've seen and said enough.
I'm just happy it's over.

Harriet and I tell our parents
we're walking home together
and we'll see them later.
As we say goodbye,
Dad pats me on the shoulder,
and I try to ignore
that he's still being weird.

"Well, that went well,"
Harriet says,
her glee at her
freedom
flying off her
like subatomic particles,
invisibly influencing me.

"Jackson is angelic
in front of his parents!"

"I know, right?" she says.
"Who was that kid?"

"So quiet.
So humble.
So polite!"

"*Yes, Mom.*
*No, Dad.*
*I'm sorry I let you down, Mom.*"

"Do you think they'll actually
take his phone away?"

"I hope so," she says.
"And the suspension.
Mr. Adamson's right:
he's lucky we're not
involving the police."

"I never thought
I'd hear you say
'Mr. Adamson is right.'"

"I never thought I'd hear
you admit you
think Benjamin
is hot."

"I haven't."

"You don't need to.
He was very sweet
in assembly. You really
like him, don't you?"

"I do," I say.
"But it's still so awkward.
We've hardly spoken
since . . . well, you know,
my period started on him.
And then he ignored me
for a week."

We're right outside the bakery,
and Harriet stops me,
her eyes wide,
her mouth open.
"Wait," she says,
a smirk on her lips.
"He gave you the big O,
and you repaid him with Aunt Flo?"

"Shh!" I hiss, nodding, shoving
her shoulder with mine
and realizing that we've never
actually talked about the details.
But she doesn't seem

to think it's disgusting.
It's more entertaining
if anything.

"Oh my god!"
she practically screams.
"This is never gonna
grow old."

Inside the bakery
we get pastries,
and as we wait
for our change,
I can feel
Harriet's shoulders
still shaking with laughter
against mine.

Out on the street,
walking home
in the afternoon sun,
just two normal girls
eating croissants,
I could cry with relief.

My best friend is beside me,
laughing about something
that previously
made me feel so disgusting.
#FriendsAreAmazing

"I can't really call you
a nun anymore,
can I?" says Harriet.

"Nuns have periods too,
Harry," I say, then snort.

And Harriet snorts too,
which makes me laugh.
And before we know it
we're both
cackling,
laugh-crying,
gasping for breath,
tears rolling down our cheeks.

We only stop
when we get to our street
and I realize that my guts
have stopped squirming,
and, for the first time
since this all started,
I feel like myself again.

Maybe laughing
is the antidote
to shame.

"Was it good?" Harriet says.

"Honestly?" I say. "Yes.
Do you think that's weird?"

"No," she says.
"I think it's great."

"Do you think it's normal
that I got my period . . .

right when . . . ?"

"I expect so. If you poke it
and there's something
waiting to come out . . .
it's going to come.
Excuse the pun."

"Harriet! You make
everything disgusting."

"That's why you love me,"
she says, brushing flakes
off her lips.

Then, as I'm in
a confessional mood,
I say, "I bit his thigh."
I wait, enjoying her face.

"It was
unbelievably
meaty."

# Dad

Harriet and I lie
on the floor in my room,
talking about
the lunar eclipse,
which is tonight.
A blood moon.
#TotallyCosmic

And we watch one of the
videos on her phone
that someone took
of us in assembly.

We're amazing.
We're warriors.
We totally nailed it.

We relive every tiny detail
and try to take in
the bigger picture.
The hilarious expression
on Mr. Adamson's face
when he read my T-shirt,
and the possibility
that what we did
might make a difference
to somebody.

Then there's a gentle knock
on my door

and I sit up and say,
"Hello?"

And Dad pokes his head
inside, sheepishly, saying,
"Is there room for three?"

Harriet nods
and shuffles over,
patting the floor
between us.

Dad reaches into
his back pocket
and says, "I got this
fixed for you."

"My phone!"
Its shiny screen is mended.
My fingers long for it,
and I reach out and take it.

"I love you,"
I say, cradling it.

"You're talking to the phone,
aren't you?" says Dad.

"Yup," I say.

"What are you watching?"
he asks.

"A video of the assembly."

Dad leans in and says,
"Great. I want to see."

I'm not sure
I want him watching,

but Harriet's already
pressing play,

and although I feel
hot with embarrassment,
at least there's nothing
invented on here.
It can't be more embarrassing
than what he's already seen.
This is all *really me*.

Dad watches, nodding,
and when it finishes,
he says, "YES! EXACTLY!"
Then he looks at me.
"You said it, girl!"

I'm so shocked,
all I can say is
"What?"

"You did. You said it.
You go, girl."

"Dad!" I groan, cringing,
"Don't call me 'girl.'"

"Should I call you
a woman now?"

"Ew, no,"
I say, but I'm so relieved
that he agrees
with what we said.
"Just be normal."

"No, thank you!" says Dad.
"Normal is boring.
I'd rather be like you."

"I thought you were
ashamed of me."

"How could I be?"

"Because of what I did."

"You didn't do anything.
I mean, I'd rather not have known
the details, but that's my problem.
I'm not ashamed of you.
I never could be."

"I thought you thought
I was disgusting."

"No," he says, touching
my cheek tenderly.
"*Society* is disgusting.
*You* are amazing.
You have amazed me
every day since the moment
you were born.
I've never been prouder."

"Dad, are you crying?"

"Maybe," Dad says,
his voice wobbling,
tears brimming.

"You two are so cute!"
Harriet cries, throwing
her arms around both of us
and squeezing us so tightly
we can hardly breathe.

Dad whispers
in my ear,
"I love you, kid."

"I love you too,"
I say, and I'm glad
for the tight squeeze,
because I'm also crying.
Then I add, quietly,
"By the way,
I sort of have a boyfriend."

And Dad laughs hotly
into my ear
and whispers, "Well,
that's just great."

# Blood Moon

Up in the tree house
Harriet and I
wait for night.
I feel floaty.
Mom was right:
being brave
really can make
your problems
melt away.
#NoWorries

I peel and portion
a tangerine and
share it with Harriet,
watching the darkness
come alive with
the light of a million stars.

We chat about the application
and what we're going to do
with our lives,
looking at the stars
and the moonrise,
the shadow of the earth
making its path
across a glowing surface.

I say,
"I think tonight

is the night for our best
moon picture yet!"

Harriet says,
"There she is!"
pointing at me.

"Huh?"

"You're back!
It's good to see you.
The good old, happy,
excited-by-the-moon,
nerdy, wonderful you."

We set up the telescope,
watching red
seep into the moon
at its edge.
Then Harriet lines it up,
closes one eye, and
puts the other
to the lens,
breathing
a long,
slow,
heavy
sigh.
"It's A-M-A-Z-I-N-G!"

I
look,
and

my mind
falls silent.

Bloodred,
impossibly lustrous,
suspended over us,
238,900 miles away.

The beauty of the blood moon
reminds me that
the universe is huge,
and we are tiny,
but so lucky,
because we get to
witness its beauty.

# Forever

I don't think
people realize that
you can take
a really good picture
of the night sky
on a phone
through a telescope.

We take a ton,
and one is amazing.
Harriet posts it
and tags me,
and then we watch
the hearts come rolling in.

And I *feel* the love,
but not online,
I mean, the real stuff,
right here,
from my best friend.

Although I hate
that the meme
will always be online,

it's amazing that some things
will be captured there
for all of time.

# Sweet Dreams

A noise wakes me
in the dead of night.
A scuffle,
a rustle,
the crack of a twig
underfoot.

I rub my eyes
and look at Harriet,
moonlit,
asleep beside me,
drooling,
her phone stuck
to her cheek.

I peel it off
and place it
beside her gently,
then lean over the boards
and peer down,
through the leaves.

"Pssst!"
a voice hisses
on the midnight breeze.

Standing there,
like a dream,
beneath the dusky
green canopy,

his face lit
by the LED
of his phone screen,
is Benjamin.

"Can I come up?"
he whispers.
"I brought pastries."

                                    I nod but put my finger
                                            to my lips.
                                      "Yes, but quietly.
                                    Harriet's asleep."

He climbs the ladder
and sits down
next to me,
smelling of his
leather jacket
and clean laundry,
and the bakery.

                                      "What time is it?"
                                              I ask.

"It's just after three."

                                    "What are you doing here?"
                                        I whisper, glancing
                                      to check that Harriet's
                                        still asleep.

"I wanted to see you,"
Benjamin says,

scooting closer,
so that both of our legs
are dangling into the tree.

"How did you find me?"

"I saw Harriet's last post.
That picture is *awesome*.
I remembered you said
you sometimes sleep
out here, and, well,
I've been awake
watching it happen."

"What happen?"
I yawn and then

he says, "Wait.
You don't know?"
He holds out his phone.

"Know what?"

"I'll show you!"
says Benjamin,
placing his thumbs
over the screen excitedly.

"Your picture of
the blood moon is trending.
Look what happens
if I google you!"

Benjamin types in my name
and I wait,

preparing for shame,
and at the same time,
dying to see.

He tilts his phone
to show me the first page.

And

.

.

.

.

The top hit
is not
the meme.

# It's just the moon.
# The beautiful full
# glorious orb
# of the bloodred moon.

And the words I see

are not

            whore

or

    slut

or

               dirty

or

    tramp

It's like:
    *this*

*amazing picture*
*of the blood moon*
*taken on a home telescope*
*by two teenagers*
*IS EVERYTHING.*

If it keeps
trending,
this could actually
put an end to the meme.
Banish it into obscurity.

"Did your sister do this?"

He shakes his head,
smiling. "It was nothing
to do with her
or me. It was all
Harriet and you."

Benjamin looks at me
with his dimpled grin,
only this time,
there's more there.

There's care,
and something that
feels like
*being seen.*

There's a crackle
between us.

And I find that I can say

what I wanted to say
to him back on the ice rink:
"I like your face."

He laughs and says,
"I like yours too."

"Do you want to
see the moon?
It's setting soon."

"Definitely," he says.
"Will it be *totally cosmic*?"

I giggle.
"Shh! Don't wake Harriet."

We shuffle
to the telescope,
and I adjust it to face
the full moon,
drifting down
toward the horizon.

Benjamin breathes in,
sharply, as he takes it in,
because that's what
happens when you
see something
awe-inspiring.

When he's seen
and seen
and seen,

he turns to me,
his eyes shining.
"What do you think?"

I ask him,
and he says,
"Beautiful,"
in a way
that makes me think
he's
maybe
talking about me.

"Um . . . Frankie?"
he says, a bit shyly.
"Do you think
you'd maybe want to,
like,
go out with me?"

"Hmm," I say,
pretending to think.
"Maybe. Let's see."

# Our Universe

As dawn is breaking,
Benjamin leaves.
"I've got rugby practice
in the morning,"
he says.

> "So, you mean now?" I say,
> looking at the time,
> as he climbs down
> the ladder.

> He waves, and grins,
> then walks across the grass.
> I turn around to lie back down

and Harriet is wide awake,
her face right in mine,
doing a giant,
stupid,
grin.

> "HARRIET!" I shriek.
> "Have you been awake
> this whole time?"

"YES," she says.
"And I heard
*everything.*
'I like your face.'"

> I pick up my pillow

and whack her with it.
"Why didn't
you say you were
friggin' awake?"

"Because," she says,
winking at me. "I know
when a girl needs *space*.
Although, my god,
the noises . . .
so sloppy . . ."

I put my hands to
my red cheeks.
"I'm so embarrassed!"

"Oh, don't be," she says, grinning.
"You two are very cute."

"Ugh," I groan.
"I can't believe you.
You're so sneaky!"

"I know!" she says proudly,
picking up her phone.
"Anyway. I practically squealed
when I heard what he said.
I thought he was
never going to leave."

She thrusts her phone
in front of me.
"We've got a ton of
new followers!"

"Amazing!"

"And look . . .
We've got a message
from Vidhi!
The planetarium wants
you and me to write a blog post
for their website about
taking home-
astronomy photographs!"

"That's so cool!" I say.

"And Vidhi says
you should check
your personal email,"
Harriet adds,
nudging me.

I open my email
and with trembling fingers
find the email from Vidhi.

I go quiet while I'm reading
and I can hear Harriet breathing,
waiting.

Vidhi says they're sorry
they suspended me.
That it wasn't fair
and that Elaine hopes
I'll come back ASAP.

Then I read the end of her email,

and I don't know whether
I'm going to laugh
or cry
or scream.

I look at Harriet,
who is watching me,
bursting.

"She read my application.
She says it's amazing.
I have an interview next week!"

"Of course you do!"
Harriet screams.
"Oh, I absolutely
knew you would!"

And although she's still
in her sleeping bag,
she dives at me,
crashing into me,
pinning me
to the warm sunlit boards
of the tree house floor,
hugging me.

Then she moves
away from me,
her freckled nose wrinkling,
"You smell of boy."

"I do not," I say.

"Well, you smell
of *something*.
How was the kissing?"

I can't help smiling.
"It was amazing."

"At least he brought these,"
she says, opening
the bag of pastries
and helping herself.
"He's all right with me."

Harriet smiles at me across
a fresh dawn sunbeam,
and in that moment,
I see my funny,
lovely,
best friend,
in all her freckled beauty.

It is a moment
overflowing with
possibility.

And right now,
right here,
with the chorus of dawn
in our sycamore tree,
that possibility is
simply
Harriet and me.

# acknowledgments

Thanks first to my passionate, meticulous editors Denise Johnston-Burt, Megan Middleton, and Susan Van Metre—it has been such a pleasure to work with you on this book. To Gráinne Clear for her sharp editorial eye, to Lindsay Warren for her insightful feedback, to Pamela Marshall and Maggie Deslaurier for the scrupulous copyedits, to Maria Middleton for the beautiful typesetting (the stars on the pages are such a lovely touch), and to Alicia Balderrama and Martha Dwyer for proofreading. Thank you again to Maria Middleton for the cover, which is bolder and more beautiful than I could have dreamed of, and to the wider team at Walker Books US and Candlewick for championing this book as it goes out into the world.

To my fabulous agent, Rachel Mann, thank you for your unflinching faith in *Blood Moon* from the moment we met—I am so lucky to work with you; and thank you to Jo Unwin and the whole team at JULA for such a warm welcome.

Jo Nadin, you brilliant woman, thank you for being an extraordinary tutor. Without you this book literally wouldn't exist. You put unapologetically high expectations on me and taught me to be bold, brave, and better. I'll never forget that. Heartfelt thanks to Steve Voake, CJ Skuse, Lucy Christopher, Janine Amos, Julia Green, David Almond, and all my classmates in the MA in Writing for Young People at Bath Spa.

Thanks to my friends, particularly my writer friends Emma Levey, Angharad James, Susanna Bailey, and

Yasmin Rahman, who read this as it grew and told me kindly what to keep and what to delete; and most particularly to Hana Tooke, Wibke Brueggemann, and Rachel Huxley—you know what you did.

Swaggers—it's hard to know what I can say about you in print, but thank you for being the most hilarious and supportive group of writers to debut with. I believe this here is some serious SWAG.

I am indebted to Caitlin Williams and her friends for letting me into their teenage world; to Caroline Ambrose and the junior judges at the Bath Children's Novel Award for their passionate responses to the book; to Briony Goffin and Amanda Rackstraw for being brilliant teachers; and to Sarah Crossan, Louise O'Neill, Jason Reynolds, and E. Lockhart for writing the kinds of YA books that made me want to write them too.

Thanks finally to my family: to Mum for talking to me about feminism from the start; to Dad, who is funnier than Frankie's dad without even trying; to my sisters for being warm, witty, and incredibly smutty; to the Crawford family for being so loving and supportive; and to my children for their endless appetite for stories. The biggest thanks to my husband, Will, for picking up the pieces when I felt broken, and always believing I could do this. Listen carefully, I shall say this only once: you were right, I *did* do it.

I owe a debt to Jon Ronson for his book *So You've Been Publicly Shamed*, and to Brené Brown, whose insightful work on shame informed the emotional core of this story. I also owe this book to the work of so many amazing feminists, especailly Caitlin Moran, Rachel Bloom, and Sophie Walker, whose funny, intelligent, brave voices helped me find mine.

# Discussion Guide

*Blood Moon* deals with topics—periods, period shaming, online abuse—that can be difficult to talk about. But *not* talking about certain things can also make them dangerous or more difficult to deal with. Author Lucy Cuthew says, "I've had heavy, painful periods since they started when I was seventeen. It was years before I found out I have endometriosis. About one in ten menstruators have this condition, but it often takes many years to be diagnosed—mostly because talking about periods is still taboo. If we can't talk about something, it's very difficult to identify a problem with it. I wrote *Blood Moon* to show what period shame looks like, to explore how harmful it can be, and to open up more conversations about it. Periods, like anything personal, can be private, but they don't need to be kept a secret. It is, after all, only blood."

The questions that follow are meant to help you think more about *Blood Moon*, but also to help you start conversations about relationships, periods, and the stigma that surrounds menstruation.

1. **What impression do you have of Harriet and Frankie's relationship? What clues in the text lead you to that conclusion?**

2. **How important are your friendships to you? What expectations do you have of your closest friends?**

3. **What are some ways you deal with fighting in a friendship?**

4. **What lengths would you go to in order to protect a friendship?**

5. **What do you think about the relationship between Frankie and Benjamin?**

6. **How do the friendships that Frankie and Benjamin have impact them?**

7. **What are some of the implied messages in this story about periods and menstruation? Where do these attitudes come from?**

8. **What are some of the ways that periods might be stigmatized in your community?**

9. **Are there any ways in which periods can be empowering?**

10. **What do you think about how Frankie handles the online bullying she experiences?**

11. **What do you think the people engaging in this bullying were trying to achieve?**

12. **How do you feel about the way the adults in this story reacted to what was happening?**

13. **What is the role of the internet in bullying and harassment?**

14. **Have you encountered positive spaces on the internet? What do those look like?**

15. **What are some of the best ways to effect change, either in your community or on a broader scale?**

16. **How would you go about uniting a group if you wanted to make a positive impact?**

17. **Are there ways that some of the conflicts in this story could have been avoided? What would those look like?**

18. **Did this novel make you think differently about anything? If so, how?**

19. **Did the fact that the novel was written in verse have an impact on your response to it?**

*Questions adapted from Blood Moon Teachers' Notes*
*© 2020 Walker Books Ltd. All Rights Reserved*
*Written by Nikki Gamble from Just Imagine Centre for*
*Excellence in Reading*